Please Don't Go

That was how I got to know the French song called *Ne me quitte pas,* which I played throughout that summer, and could never have enough of. *Ne me quitte pas* is Tréguinec, is my first experience of love, is that summer of my sixteenth year, and I've no doubt when I'm thirty it will all come back just as clearly when I hear that song. We sat in Mic's room playing the record the whole of that warm stuffy rainy afternoon; we put the song on again and again, until Mic's room became a magic outpost cut off from the world.

"A brilliant evocation of summer relationships." Horn Book

Please Don't Go

Peggy Woodford

AVON
PUBLISHERS OF BARD, CAMELOT, DISCUS, EQUINOX AND FLARE BOOKS

AVON BOOKS
A division of
The Hearst Corporation
959 Eighth Avenue
New York, New York 10019

Copyright © 1972 by Peggy Woodford.
Published by arrangement with E. P. Dutton and Company, Inc.
Library of Congress Catalog Card Number: 72-89840.

ISBN: 0-380-00221-3

First Avon Printing, January, 1975.
Second Printing

AVON TRADEMARK REG. U.S. PAT. OFF. AND
FOREIGN COUNTRIES, REGISTERED TRADEMARK—
MARCA REGISTRADA, HECHO EN CHICAGO, U.S.A.

Printed in the U.S.A.

For Alison and Frances

1

The very first time the Menards took me down to the
beach at Tréguinec I noticed him. Amongst the
hordes of yapping French people he sat silently reading a paperback. He was very brown and had black
wavy hair. Perhaps he felt my glance, because he
looked up suddenly in my direction. His eyes were
pale, pale blue. They looked strange in his brown
face; I had never seen anyone at home as brown as
he was. I looked away quickly. It was the first time
in my life a man had caught my attention so fully,
and it made me feel a little tense.

Though there were at least three large families in
our group, Mic only introduced me to two people, a
girl called Françoise and a boy called Joël. Françoise
was slim and pretty and wore those neat French jeans
which fit so well. She made me feel a lump; my jeans
were baggy and had generous turnups owing to their
length. Everyone talked fast, too fast for me to follow.
Suddenly Mic, Françoise and Joël set off up the beach;
it was Joël who came back for me and said slowly and
clearly,

'Come on. We're going to play ping-pong.' He made
batting movements, and smiled encouragingly. He
had wild red hair and freckles, and was tall and
gangly; he was obviously a year or two older than me.
He pointed: 'We play over there, in that café.' Mic

and Françoise had already gone inside. I glanced back at the beautiful man as we walked up the beach; he had stopped reading, and was talking now to Mic's mother, Madame Menard.

The café consisted of a large room, with the ping-pong table at one end, some bar-football tables in the middle, and an assorted collection of café tables at the other end near a zinc-topped counter. The barman sold everything: ices, coffee, booze, stamps, sweets, and those smelly French cigarettes. The whole place reeked of them and I must say I liked it.

The barman wore a T-shirt with the name Elvis Presley stretched across his fat chest. The T-shirt was faded and full of holes. The man smiled at me and said something in a hoarse gravelly voice; I smiled weakly back and muttered, *'Anglaise.'*

'Ah. *Anglaise,'* he said as if it wasn't obvious, and I loved Jean from then on. He poured out a glass of stuff called Pschitt-Orange, and presented it to me saying, *'Bien venue à Tréguinec.'* He scratched himself as he watched me drink it, a smile of approval on his face.

'C'est bon ça.'

'Oui.' The orange juice was indeed delicious, and he wouldn't let me pay for it. The table was free now, and the four of us started to play. Ping-pong is one of the few games I'm good at, so I began to feel distinctly more cheerful. Jean shouted hoarse encouragement. I learned later he was supposed to charge us for using the ping-pong table, but he never did.

While we were playing, Jean's radio crackled and blared. He leant over the bar watching us, humming to himself in between comments. The music changed to a tune that was sad and powerful; Jean held up his finger and said, 'Ah, *mes enfants,* listen to this. The best song in the world.'

'We know it,' said Françoise. 'It's *Ne me quitte pas.'* She was unimpressed. *'C'est vieux ça.'*

8

'You have no ears, Françoise,' he said. Then his radio started crackling and blurping so much that the song was inaudible. Jean twiddled the knobs and swore but the noise got worse; he switched it off angrily.

And so it happened that in my first afternoon at Tréguinec I saw the beautiful man, I met Joël, and I heard *Ne me quitte pas* for the first time; all three in their different ways were going to change my life.

The Menards were my exchange-family; Mic, really Marie-Claire, had just stayed with me in London and now I was staying in their summer place in Brittany for the first time. Their home was in Paris, and Monsieur Menard worked for the Government. Mic wasn't very clear at what. My father is a doctor. The Menards had five children, which I was discovering is a moderate family by French standards. Joël's family, the Jouberts, were six children, Joël at sixteen was the eldest; the youngest was a baby known as Pish. Mic was fifteen, like me, and was followed by Gervaise, Angélique, Patrice and Etienne. The last two were dreadful little boys, worse than my own little brothers.

There was another large family who spent the summer at Tréguinec called Lamartine; I never sorted them out. Françoise de la Tour was the youngest of her family, and was staying with her grandmother. She told me her sisters were married and did not come to Tréguinec any more.

'They go to the South of France,' she said. 'It's more amusing. I'm going next year. Tréguinec is boring when you get older.' Though I liked Françoise, she made me feel inferior. She even looked after her nails properly; mine always looked as if I'd used them to scrape the dog's dish.

The Menards had two little houses in one garden, just above the beach up a steep path. The houses were old two-storey granite cottages at right angles to each other; fruit trees grew trained against the walls. If a Breton wall was sunny, it had fruit not flowers growing up it. The garden was full of fleshy green flowers, unknown to me, which I later learned were artichokes.

One of the little houses was slightly smaller, and I think had once been a barn or a stable. We slept in it, above the dining-room and primitive kitchen, an arrangement of calor gas rings behind a curtain. Every floor in those houses was gritty with sand. I don't think anyone ever swept them, so it didn't matter how much mess we made. We all slept in Breton beds, which are like cupboards built into the walls or eaves, and curtained. Mine was the most beautiful. There was carving all over the wooden frame, red-checked curtains to draw, and plenty of room inside to sit up and read or talk. Right from the start Mic and Angélique would join me in my cupboard bed, and we would talk at night for hours. Monsieur and Madame and the boys slept in the other house, and never heard us. Some nights we crept down and pinched food to eat in our hideout, but there was never much to pinch. Madame bought fresh stuff every day, most of which got eaten. I adored the smells in that little house; of garlic cooking in oil and butter, of fresh bread, of chocolate warming in the morning for our breakfast.

The morning after I arrived was clear and hot, so we had breakfast outside at a battered tin table, and drank our chocolate from bowls. Then we ran down to the beach; the tide was high so we bathed at once in the sparkling green water. No bathe was ever better than the morning bathe when the tide was high. While I was in the water, I saw the beautiful man appear at the top of the beach; he stared hard as if looking for someone, spoke briefly to Françoise, and then disappeared again. I wanted to ask Mic who he was, but she was so sharp it wasn't worth risking the teasing that would inevitably result.

There was much about Mic I didn't like and much

10

I did; my feelings just about balanced each other out. I was stuck with her and she with me; our parents had fixed up our exchange and we just had to get on with it. Mic once said slowly to me, looking at me assessingly from under her long eyelashes, her head tipped back,

'*Quelquefois je t'aime et quelquefois je te déteste.*'

'Snap.'

She was very cool, was Marie-Claire Menard. '*Je suis égoiste, moi,*' she said, proudly, and I envied her having thought of herself that way. It had never even occurred to me to wonder whether I was an egoist or not. But I began to think about myself that first summer in France.

2

France smelt so different, lovely strange scents.
Houses smelt different, buses smelt different, even the
beach did. Most of all, the café smelt different from
every English café I had ever been in. As I waited
with Mic for the ping-pong table to be free I tried to
work out why. The smell of French cigarettes, of coffee,
the faint sweet buttery smell of the croissants lying in
a basket on the bar; those were obvious. The café was
built entirely of wood, and sand brought in on people's
bare feet was thick on the floor. Maybe this all went to
make the café smell so special. The smells of things
have always mattered to me; perhaps other people
don't notice them so much.

'Now, I am going to challenge the English cham-
pion,' said Jean. 'Mic, go and be barman for me.'
Mic stationed herself behind the bar on his stool, and
Jean and I started to play. Though he was fat and
quite old, he was very good, and I could see he was
going to beat me hollow.

'Bonjour, Antoine,' he said to someone who had
come in behind me. 'Mic will serve you.'

When we changed sides after the next point I saw
who it was: the man who made my stomach lurch.
So he was called Antoine. He bought some cigarettes
from Mic, who was being off-hand and business-like,
but I could see she was enjoying herself. Antoine

13

then watched us play, tapping his teeth with his sunglasses. I served miles off the table and felt my face turning bright red. Jean began to tut-tut. I longed for our game to be over; I hated to be watched by anyone at all, let alone this unsettling man. I heard him say to Mic, 'Who is that?' His voice was flat, sounding very bored.

'It's my English exchange.' She did not give my name, and I made my only good smash for five minutes in my annoyance.

'That's better,' said Jean.

Then a woman's voice started calling outside, 'Antoine, Antoine, *je suis prête, allons-y.*' He left immediately. The woman was in a small Renault with a suitcase on its roof rack; Antoine got in and they drove off. I felt depressed.

'We stop,' said Jean, and pinched my cheek. He had the kindest way of doing it. 'Off,' he said to Mic, who was sitting very much at home behind the bar. 'Off.'

'A Pschitt-Orange for payment,' said Mic and dodged out of the door when he chased her. I followed her on to the beach, and sat down at the edge of the crowd of families which by now had gathered. They always sat in the same place on the beach and dug themselves in for the day. Even when they went up for lunch, things were left on the beach until they came back. They really lived on it, and the women never stopped talking. Summer after summer the same families came, mostly from Paris. I wondered why London families didn't do the same. Perhaps some did, but I did not know any. As far as I could see neither the Menards nor the other families were at all rich. About the same as us, and I can just imagine what my father would say if I suggested he bought a house by the sea.

I was ravenous by the time Mic and I drifted back to the Menards' for lunch. Madame had spent most of the morning gassing on the beach so I expected

14

lunch to be sketchy. But that was another thing I learned about French life; our three-course lunch was all prepared at the last minute and it was delicious. I began to feel the French had a lot to teach us; I wrote this to my father and he replied he was glad to see I was becoming biased.

After lunch we were supposed to have a siesta, but since Madame rested in the other house, Mic and I slipped out to the beach without her noticing. The beach was almost deserted at this hour, except for a group of little boys in the charge of a priest. The priest had his cassock hitched up showing fat white legs, but he ran as fast as the boys did. They were playing volleyball; the net was put up by the Jouberts, and the orphans were allowed to use it every day after lunch. When Mic said that the boys were orphans I was surprised; these noisy little devils weren't in the least like the sad white-faced beings I'd imagined.

'Bonjour, Marie-Claire,' said the priest. 'Vous voulez jouer?'

'Bonjour, Monsieur le curé. Non, merci.' Then she indicated me. 'Je vous présente Mary Meredith.' I shook sandy hands with the priest.

'Vous êtes anglaise, Mademoiselle?'

'Oui.'

The orphans stared at me as if I was a Martian. Then, at a loss for further conversation, the priest clapped his hands and they all rushed back to their game.

I left Mic giggling with Françoise and went off exploring by myself. I climbed round the headland; beyond it was a small sandy beach, quite empty; it was so pretty and private I wondered why our crowd didn't use it instead of the large beach. I lay down on the soft smooth sand and closed my eyes in the hot sun. Almost at once a voice shouted at me and made me jump violently.

A grey-haired man came up and said angrily, 'This beach is private. Didn't you see the sign?'

I understood him but my French deserted me. He said something else which I didn't catch, so I stammered,

'*Je m'excuse. Je suis anglaise.*'

He answered me in perfect English. 'This beach is private property. If you want to walk along the cliffs there's a public path above there.' He pointed up the low cliffs. I could see a modern house half hidden behind shrubs and pine trees.

'I'm sorry. Nobody warned me.'

'Good day.'

As I left I saw him go to a boathouse and open the doors; he began to drag out a fibreglass dinghy. There was a large motorboat anchored off shore, which I supposed must have been his. I asked Joël later who he was.

'Baron Auguste de la Parmentière. Was he rude to you?' Joël had bright, intelligent green eyes.

'Fairly.'

'He's got a nasty reputation. Very unfriendly. The locals don't like him at all. Apparently he lives here during the winter as well.'

As we talked I suddenly noticed Antoine out of the corner of my eye; he was sitting quite near me, reading a book. I hadn't seen him come; my heart did a somersault. He was alone; the woman he had driven off with that morning was nowhere to be seen. I wondered who he was and where he came from; and how he fitted into the Menard-Joubert-Lamartine group. He consumed my attention. It was more than curiosity; I felt an interest so strong that it used the whole of me, like being cold does. The feeling surprised me; and I couldn't control it. I wanted to look at him, but he was so close I did not dare.

Madame Menard moved up to Antoine and started to talk brightly to me. I couldn't catch all they were saying, but the phrase 'dinner tomorrow' cropped up twice, so it seemed Antoine had been invited to the Menards. That evening Madame Menard mentioned he was coming, because his wife Marie had had to return to Paris to look after her mother, who was seriously ill. So the woman had been his wife. I wished I had looked more closely at her.

The invitation to Antoine made it easier for me to ask Mic who he was when we sat talking late that night in my Breton bed. Mic had slipped down to the dining-room and stolen a piece of the cake Madame Menard had made for our dessert to celebrate Monsieur's arrival that afternoon from Paris. We divided the cake up carefully.

'I swiped the lot,' said Mic. 'However little I took my mother would have noticed so I thought I might as well pinch it all—the row will be justified.' She opened her mouth wide and swallowed her lot in one go. The cake was delicious, tasting of butter and coffee, like no English cake I'd ever had.

'Who is this Antoine who's coming to dinner to-morrow?'

Mic gave me a quick look. 'He came to buy cigarettes in the café this morning.'

'Oh, that one. While I was playing against Jean, you mean.'

'That one.' There was a pause, before Mic added lightly, 'Don't you think he's good-looking?' She used the phrase *beau-type*.

'Yes, I suppose he is in a way.'

'He's not *sympathique* though. He makes you feel a fool by being cold and sarcastic.'

'That's your specialty—you ought to get on well with him.' I dodged Mic's fist, and was smothered with a pillow instead. When the turmoil subsided, I asked, 'What does he do? Does he live in Paris?' No job I could imagine fitted Antoine. Mic shrugged.

'He lives in Paris, but I don't know what he does.' She implied by her tone she didn't care either. But she was so off-hand about him I wondered if she felt the same as I did. I didn't like the idea.

17

'His wife Marie is very beautiful,' said Mic gloomily. 'She used to be a mannequin, they say.'

'Does Antoine have a house at Tréguinec too?'

'They have a farmhouse inland a little. It's big and very beautiful. I'll take you there one day.' Mic rarely enthused about anything, so it must be beautiful. I hoped we'd go soon, but said nothing more; I yawned instead and pretended to be very sleepy. Mic left me, and I lay and thought for ages. I tried to understand why this man I didn't know should fascinate me so, but did not find a good reason. I began to suspect I had fallen in love for the first time in my life.

I have long fair hair, slightly wavy, and though the rest of me is not up to much, even my enemies will admit that my hair is something special. It's thick, and the yellow colour looks almost pink when it's washed. When I get depressed about my bulges, or my lack of prettiness in general, I go and look at my hair in a mirror, and it cheers me up.

The next morning I decided to wash my hair so that it would look its best for Antoine. I slunk off to the village shop beyond the café and bought a small bottle of brilliant green shampoo. I was holding its luscious colour against the sun when a voice made me jump.

'La belle Anglaise.' It was Jean, standing in the door of his café.

'I'm not belle.'

He smiled at me in a way that was specially nice.

'Your hair is beautiful, truly beautiful. I've forgotten your name, tell me again.'

'Mary Meredith.'

'Mary Meredith.' The way he said Meredith made us both laugh. 'Meridit . . . it's impossible to say, this name! But Mary, that's easy. Mary, would you like an ice-cream? They are free today.' He winked at me.

'No, please, I'll get fat.'

'A tiny, tiny one then.'

'I'm too fat already.'

'Tiny.' I gave in, and was presented with a whopper. 'Voilà. It's right for girls of your age to be plump.'

I thought of objectionable aunts who talked about puppy fat. Jean's face was kind; my aunts always looked as if they hoped the puppy-fat would be permanent. Anyway, the ice-cream was worth it.

'It's delicious. English ice-cream never tastes like this.'

'Ahh.' Jean stared dreamily over the sea, as if he was looking across it into England itself. 'Angleterre. I have been once on a day trip from Calais.' Somehow it surprised me to hear that the French actually took day trips to England. 'We went to Dovaire. We saw the Chateau de Dovaire, and drank disgusting tea like brown ink.'

He laughed, shaking all over. 'Brown ink,' he repeated. I laughed too, because his laugh was so infectious. We were hooting away when Mic appeared, sent to buy cigarettes for her father. She looked peeved when she saw us.

'What are you laughing at?'

'Le Chateau de Dovaire,' said Jean, and we were off again.

'Silly fools,' muttered Mic. 'Everyone's stupid today.' She was in a particularly bad mood because her father had set her some holiday work to do, and she had not even started it. He had asked her about it this morning, and his treatment of her made me see where Mic got her sarcastic tongue from.

Jean tried in vain to cheer her up. She bought two packets of Caporal, and said as she left, 'I'd poison these if I could.' I continued up to the Menards' cottages to wash my hair.

'Where are you going?' asked Mic sourly. She's the sort of girl who, having left you to sink or swim, looks

19

aggrieved if you swim. I was becoming independent at Tréguinec, and it annoyed her.

'I must write to my parents.'

'You can do it on the beach.'

'I'd rather not, I'll never get a letter finished that way.'

'I never write to my parents,' said Mic crushingly. 'You're a fool.'

'So you said already.' I enjoy writing to my parents, so I let her think what she liked. I went back to the cottages, washed my hair in more or less cold water, and sat at the table outside the dining-room window to let it dry and write my letter. My hair smelt sweet and felt lighter on my head; freshly-washed hair is very pleasant.

It turned out that Madame had asked Joël's parents to dinner as well; she had obviously decided to make a party of it. I asked Joël if he was coming too and he said no rather gloomily.

Madame left the beach early to prepare the food, and as she left suggested to Mic that she and I might follow soon to help her. I noticed that Mic never did a single thing to help her mother; when I mentioned this fact to her, she shrugged her shoulders and said French girls never did. They all used Madame Menard as a slave, and she didn't seem to mind. But she would fly into a rage if they didn't do their homework, or if they forgot something like a Latin verb or a historical fact. All the children were supposed to do their *devoirs* before they went to the beach in the morning. Mic occasionally did hers at night.

I swept the dining-room floor for Madame and collected a bucketful of sand, shells, seaweed and other marine objects. I left quite a few shells in the corners, because I thought they suited the room. Then I made a table decoration of great blown artichoke flowers, surrounded by greenish wild flowers, all arranged in a pewter bowl.

'That's very beautiful,' said Madame, looking at me

as if she saw me for the first time. 'Look at this, Marie-Claire, you never make beautiful artistic things like this.' Mic looked murderous, and I don't blame her. She said nothing then, but later on admitted she thought my arrangement was good. We laid the table with the Breton pottery they always used, and wooden-handled knives and forks.

'*Charmante,*' said Monsieur, raising his eyebrows in surprise. His eyebrows were like thick black caterpillars, but his head was almost completely bald. He was tall and thin, and rarely smiled. He smiled now, a sudden warm friendly smile. 'And the floor has been swept. *Incroyable.*'

He was holding a newspaper, and he showed us a photograph. 'The general and me,' he said in a mocking voice. There he was, shaking hands with a general, slightly bent and smiling.

'You look ridiculous, Papa,' said Mic. 'As if you're about to eat out of his hands.'

'The truth is he eats out of mine.'

Madame laughed. 'The photograph in *France-Soir* last month was better.'

Monsieur put on an old straw hat, tipped up his chin and assumed the expression of a haughty woman, and did a little dance. 'I must think of my public,' he announced, and posed with one hip out like a beauty queen. We were all laughing when a violent hissing noise came from behind the curtain, followed by a stench of burning milk.

'*Mon dieu, le déssert!*' wailed Madame, and fled.

Mic and I went down to the beach for a final dip; I tied my hair up carefully.

'I thought you liked getting your hair wet,' said Mic, slyly.

'Not always.'

'*Pas toujours, pas toujours!*' Mic imitated my French accent, and minced away. For a moment she looked very like her father. I threw a handful of wet sand at her, which landed with a satisfactory thwack

on her bottom. Mic looked very surprised, and even upset; she did not like being teased. She had her bathe
at the far end of the beach.

The sun set, facing straight into Tréguinec between
the two headlands. On a fine sunny evening like this
one, it was like bathing in liquid gold; both the air
and the surface of the sea dazzled you. In the evening
the smell of everything on the beach was heightened;
the seaweed smelt more salty and rank, the scent of
Gauloises was noticeable, whiffs of gorse scent came
from the cliffs. I floated on a lilo, happy, and for
some reason I thought about my future. Deep inside
me I had a secret ambition to be an actress; though
I hadn't acted I suspected I would be good. I never
told anyone about my ambition; it was too important to
talk about yet. But whatever happened I had decided
to go to University first.

I was standing drying myself, still thinking about
my future, when a voice said, *'Bonsoir, Mademoiselle,'* at my elbow, shattering my thoughts and making me jump.

'I'm sorry I disturbed you.' It was the priest whom
I had seen with the orphans. My French deserted me,
England had been so intensely in my mind. The priest
was tongue-tied and very embarrassed; he found it
difficult to meet my eyes.

'I was going to ask you to do us a great favour.'

'Bien sûr.'

He had a large red rubber ball in his hands which
he kept pressing, or bouncing smartly on the beach.

'It is this. I wondered whether you would be so
kind as to come and talk English to my orphans.' He
had to repeat this sentence twice, because he put it in
such involved French I could not follow it. 'They
speak a little English but with such bad accents it
would be a great pleasure for them to hear an English
voice.' He beamed at me, and threw the ball in the
air, catching it neatly. 'Only once or twice, of course,
that would be quite sufficient. Just to hear your ac-

cent. They have an exam in English next year.' I noticed how badly bitten the priest's fingernails were; the sleeves of his soutane were frayed.

'Of course I'll come and talk English. Any time.'

'Thank you, thank you, Mademoiselle; perhaps next week.' He was so pleased, he looked like a little boy himself. 'My boys will be delighted. Thank you.' And off he went, bouncing the red ball ahead of him as he ran up the beach. I was flattered he had asked me, but preferred not to think about the ordeal of facing those boys. What on earth would I talk to them *about?* It was an awful prospect.

'What did the priest want?' It was Mic, in a better humour.

'He asked me to talk English to his boys.'

'Rather you than me.' We raced to the cottages, to tidy up before dinner. I wondered what to wear. I hadn't brought many clothes with me; not that I had much to bring. I'm always putting off getting new clothes until I grow thinner, and I don't grow thinner. My mother isn't much help, because she likes the sort of clothes I don't. And my father wouldn't notice if I wore jeans on my head.

Madame called from the kitchen, 'Marie-Claire! Put a pretty dress on; your green one.' Mic immediately looked rebellious.

'Why?'

'Because I say so.'

'Just for Antoine—what's the point?'

'He's a guest. You will put a dress on.'

Mic stormed up the wooden stairs to our room, making a loud banging with her feet. Madame looked murderous, and hot from cooking. I escaped upstairs as quickly and quietly as I could.

Mic was tearing open drawers and rummaging through them. 'I'll wear a dress all right.'

'Will this do?' I held out the 'best' dress I had brought unwillingly with me.

'Of course.' She barely glanced at it. She was busy

23

trying on a black crepe evening blouse which had obviously been her mother's. It scooped so low down in front she had to take her bra off. Then she wound the Breton coverlet off her bed round herself, and kept it up with a tight wide leather belt; she surveyed the result with satisfaction. She looked wild, like a gipsy, but very good I thought enviously. Mic had a trim figure; most French girls have. They don't seem to be afflicted with thighs the way English girls are. I looked, and felt a frump in my cotton dress. It was too tight across my bottom and out of fashion.

'I hate my dress.' I could have cried.

Mic looked at me with attention, now she had dressed herself. 'I hate it too.' She opened her half of the carved Breton wardrobe; the doors were thickly carved with leaves and fruit and stocky people. 'Would you like to wear one of mine? There's a loose one which will fit you.' It was plain dark green with insets of white; I had already admired it when she wore it in London. It was so well cut it made me look quite slim. Mic examined me with narrowed eyes.

'You can have it. Green doesn't suit me.'

Before I could thank her she started to dance energetically round the room, to make sure the bedspread was safely anchored. 'This get-up will annoy my mother.' She was right. But being crafty, she didn't appear until Antoine and the Jouberts had already arrived, and a full-scale row was unlikely.

'Bonsoir, Gipsy Rose Lee,' said Antoine, laughing at her. His pronunciation of the name was so clumsy I suspected he couldn't speak much English. 'Will you read my hand?'

'If you cross my palm with silver.' Mic held Antoine's hand close to her eyes. 'I see love, tragedy, despair and death,' she announced dramatically.

'Is that all? How disappointing. Sure you can't see a murder or two, and possibly a spell on a convict island?'

Monsieur handed round glasses of vermouth, and

everyone talked noisily. I began to enjoy the party; though I couldn't follow all the conversations around me, I gathered enough not to feel too left out. I was put next to Monsieur Joubert at table, and Antoine was down at the far end, next to Madame Menard. I could watch him without anyone noticing, because Madame talked most of the time to the table at large, smiling her charming smile. I only really listened to the conversation if Antoine was leading it.

'Telepathy has no scientific proof,' said Antoine in the half darkness before candles were lit. 'I don't believe in it.'

'Nonsense, several things have happened to me that couldn't have any other explanation.' Everyone started to give examples.

Antoine shouted them down. 'Sheer coincidence, that's a much more interesting thing. The power of coincidence. How often does it affect our lives? Again and again.' I thought this was a good point, and desperately tried to work out something to say, but by the time I was ready the discussion had switched to some story of Madame Joubert's. I reached for my glass of wine to console myself for the wasted effort, and spilt half of it down the front of that beautiful green dress.

'You must be drunk,' said Mic.

Madame came upstairs with me and took the dress away to soak it. That was the last I saw of it, because Mic never told her mother she'd given it to me. I had to wear my boring dress after all, and it made me feel younger, fatter, and more hideous. Life was very unfair. Down below through the wooden floor-boards I heard shrieks of laughter, and the happy voices of people enjoying themselves.

'No, no, that bit was in *Les Vacances de Monsieur Hulot*.'

'No, it was in *Mon Oncle*.'

'Imitate him again, Philippe.' Gales of laughter at something Monsieur Menard was doing.

I felt outside it all, and a dense wave of homesickness overcame me. I longed passionately for my own home, for my mother, father and brothers, and for a language and a habit of living I didn't have to make a continuous effort over. I longed for London, for our house in Clapham, on the edge of the Common. I longed for it with all my being. I went to the window, and leant out of it, breathing the sweet sea air; for a moment I felt muddled, as if I was leaning out of my bedroom window at home and breathing the sea air instead of the stale shallow air of London. Then I could hear, through the noise of the party, the sound of waves on pebbles and rocks. I could see lights in Jean's café; a cat miaowed in the lane, and a car light flashed on a headland miles away. As I stood staring out, I found a tube ticket in my pocket: Clapham South to Trafalgar Square. That was the trip to the National Gallery with Mic, only ten days before. It seemed like a year ago, on another planet.

Through the hubbub below came Antoine's voice clearly.

'What's happened to *la petite Anglaise?*'

London and home faded, and what mattered was Brittany, now. I felt absurdly pleased he should have noticed my absence, though the pleasure was lessened slightly when I heard him add, 'What's her name? I've forgotten.'

'Mary Meredith.'

'Mary, Marie. By the way, Marie says would you like to . . .' I didn't hear any more because the noise increased; I brushed my hair and went down the stairs, and met Madame Menard at the foot.

'I was just coming up to get you,' she said. 'What a pretty dress!'' She smiled, to cover up the fact that she didn't mean it. She clapped her hands. 'Now, who wants *crème* and who wants *gâteau* for pudding?'

After dinner, Mic, Gervaise, Angélique and I played the record-player at one end of the dining-room, and improvised dances. The grown-ups sat outside by the low window, and drank brandy. Moths bumped against the lights. Antoine came in while we were arguing about which record to put on.

'Enough *yé-yé*. Let's have some proper music. Have you any Jacques Brel, Mic?'

'Not here. All my records are in Paris. These are Gervaise's.' Antoine looked through the pile of battered records quickly.

'Gervaise, Gervaise, your taste. I am in the mood for Jacques Brel. I'll fetch some of my records, it won't take a moment in the car.' He looked at Mic and me. 'Like to come for the ride?'

We followed him out of the house, Mic muttering to herself as she hitched her bedspread more safely round her waist, 'One can't dance to Jacques Brel. What a bore Antoine is with his enthusiasms.'

'Are you abducting my girls?' called out Monsieur Menard.

'Only for a few days,' said Antoine.

'Make sure they clean their teeth and say their prayers, then.'

I giggled, but Mic looked stony. Antoine and Monsieur went on bantering until Mic got into Antoine's car and slammed the door.

It was one of those sardine-tin Renaults and we drove like the clappers to his house. I thought the car was going to turn over as we bumped and twisted down the narrow drive. We stopped with a jerk outside a big silent farmhouse. Antoine led the way through the dark house, putting on a few lights; it was all panelled inside, full of carved Breton furniture and old-fashioned pictures. The air smelt sweet and almost oily. Cats appeared from every room, all kinds of cats; they padded after Antoine miaowing.

'So many cats,' I said.

'They're Marie's.' He looked at the cats with dislike. 'I expect I forgot to feed them this evening.'

'You're a cruel master,' said Mic. She treated Antoine with familiarity, but I could see she was nervous of him. He wasn't quite in the grown-ups' bracket, because he was so much younger than her parents and the Jouberts. This made him approachable, but not easily.

He fetched the records, and then stopped in the kitchen to open tins of cat food. The cats wound themselves round him, screeching. 'Blasted animals.' I watched him put the food out on to various plates. He was really a very beautiful man. His house was mysterious and beautiful too. He snapped off lights and we followed him out to the car. As we climbed into the Renault Mic's skirt came off, revealing dark blue knickers, school-type. Mic rewrapped the bedspread looking unconcerned.

'You're a naughty girl,' said Antoine.

'*Merci.*' Mic smiled to herself.

After a pause I said, 'Your house is beautiful.'

'Yes. But all winter long I feel it hanging like a weight on me, demanding to be visited.' Since feeding the cats his expression had been sullen; his tone was bitter.

We drove back in silence, and when we got back Antoine immediately put on one of his records. Since he had made such a point of collecting them, and obviously liked this singer I'd never heard of, I listened very carefully. I was disappointed; the songs seemed nothing special. Yet Antoine sat smiling to himself as he listened. I wondered what I had missed, and decided to get to know the record better.

'Would you lend me your record for a few days?'

'Of course.' He sounded surprised, even pleased. I tried to think of something more to say to him, something to keep the conversation going, but as usual I couldn't think of anything except obvious things like the weather, so I said nothing and he moved away to talk to Monsieur Menard.

'Philippe—tell me about the scandal over our dear president's wife . . .' They went off into a corner.

Sometimes I wonder whether I'll ever be able to

chatter gaily to people I don't know very well. At the moment all I can do is stand in dense silence, my mind growing more like a pudding each minute. I had so much wanted to talk to Antoine, just to get to know him; to talk easily about nothing special. I hated myself for being so gauche. And when I felt gauche all my other faults seemed to stand out: my plumpness, my shabby nails, the spot on my chin. They all signalled their presence like beacons. I have come to the firm conclusion that being a teenager is in many ways a misery. Though the idea of growing old is frightening, when I think of the hell of being fifteen, I'd rather be grown-up; surely grown-ups don't go through the same agonies. Madame Menard has quite a pot belly, but I'm sure she isn't conscious of it and worried about it all the time. In fact, I know she isn't because Mic said to her, 'You're getting fat,' and she said, 'I know,' as if she was quite pleased about it. Then Mic said, 'You ought to slim. Men don't like fat women,' and Madame just laughed at her. Anyway slimming is very hard work, because people conspire against you all the time to weaken your already weak will; and parents are the worst because they are so used to pumping food into you that they find it hard to accept that they've overdone it.

Mic came up looking very annoyed. 'Maman says we must go to bed.' The grandfather clock said it was eleven thirty, so I could see Madame's point. 'How can we possibly sleep anyway with all the noise going on?' No one took any notice of her, so she repeated loudly, 'I can't sleep with a din going on.'

'Marie-Claire,' said her father, breaking off his talk with Antoine, 'I know for a fact that you have perfected a system of deafness on demand; now is a good time to use it.' Sarcasm in French sounds better (or worse, depending which end you're on) than in any other language. Mic flounced off to bed, and I wished

29

everyone good night, shaking hands all round as is the custom. Antoine's hand was cold and firm.

We did not feel at all sleepy, so we played cards in my bed with the curtains drawn. We heard the party below break up, and Monsieur and Madame went off to bed in the other house. Mic crept downstairs and came back with a bottle containing a few inches of wine, and a glass. We drank it feeling happily wicked.

A stone hit Mic's window, then another. We looked out and there was Joël. 'I thought you'd still be up,' he whispered.

'Come and drink some wine,' said Mic; and Joël crept up the stairs. Whispering and laughing together, we finished the wine.

'Let's go for a walk,' said Joël. 'The moon is so bright.' We managed to leave silently, and went down the path to the beach.

'Let's go on the Baron's land,' said Mic. 'Since we never can in the daytime. Just for a lark.'

We clambered off over the cold slippery rocks. The tide was out, and had left behind acres of whispering, crackling seaweed. It seemed to make much more noise than it did in the daytime; I kept imagining horrible monsters flexing their muscles under those mounds of wet seaweed. I avoided treading on any. A sucking, thudding sound made us stop in our tracks until we realized it was the sea, sucking and flowing through some hole in the rock. Suck, thud, whoosh, suck, thud, whoosh. It was eerie. Those sea anemones like shiny brown breasts made little sucking noises too, and gleamed as if they were watching us. Bladderwrack popped under our feet occasionally, and we jumped and giggled every time one of us dislodged a stone. Sounds carried so clearly; we could hear a dog bark and growl across the bay as if it was only a hundred feet away.

We rounded the headland. There was the private beach, and the boat-house, all locked up. The sea had left the sand smooth, unmarked by feet. We crept along a small rabbit path above the rocks, well shielded by gorse bushes and other prickly sorts of growth. Our clothes kept catching in the brambles and thorns, so our progress was fairly slow. When I trod in some stinging nettles I began to long for my bed. We saw no sign of life whatsoever; no lights, no sounds.

The wild bushes began to look organized; we were walking round a hedge of gorse and hawthorn, carefully planted both to screen and keep people out. It looked as if it would keep us out too, unless we forced our way through it. I suggested going home, and Mic immediately scoffed at me.

'We've got this far, let's at least get in.' Mic chose a thinnish part of the hedge, which luckily straddled a ditch, and we crawled in great discomfort down this. At the end of it we emerged in a rhododendron shrubbery, and we gathered under a particularly large, bushy, and mercifully thornless bush. Through the leaves we could pick out the house, about fifty yards away up a sloping lawn. It was built very low, hugging the earth, a modern house full of glass set diagonally.

'Very snug, in winter gales,' whispered Joël. 'Those windows would catch the sun but be out of the prevailing wind, angled like that. Very ingenious. The Baron lives here all the year round, *on dit*.' I wish English could reproduce the full flavour of '*on dit*', but 'it is said' and 'they say' aren't right, because neither is impersonal yet personal enough; '*on dit*' includes the speaker, but casually.

There were lights on behind curtains, but no sign of anyone. We sat and watched the house for a while.

'I'm getting bored with this. Let's explore a bit,' said Joël. We were just about to break cover when a glass door opened and out came a man, smoking. He stood on the terrace, gazing out to sea, his cigar glinting red when he drew on it.

'It's the Baron,' whispered Mic. It was the man I

had seen on the beach. He was wearing a long dark robe, probably his dressing-gown. We could hear music through the open door, unfamiliar whining music which went on and on with a snakey sort of rhythm.

'Indian music,' said Joël. The sound of the waves breaking on the rocks did not go very well with it. We watched the Baron watching the sea. Then Mic stepped back on to a dead branch, and the loud snapping noise made the Baron look our way; he started to stroll towards us.

'*Fiche le camp!*' hissed Mic, and we did. We eventually found ourselves near the top of the headland; there was a drive which led to Tréguinec. We strolled along it until Mic said something silly which started us laughing. We laughed until we were hysterical, rolling about on the grassy verge, kicking our legs in the air, trying to keep our laughter quiet but not succeeding. Hoo, hoo, hoo went Joël, heh, heh, heh cackled Mic, and I groaned because I had laughed so much it hurt. Slowly we sobered up, and sat, tired now, on the grass. Goodness knows what the time was; at least two o'clock, I guessed. I shivered; there were high clouds scudding across the moon.

Behind us was a large flat field which looked as if it was used for some special purpose. The centre was worn and the grass all round it swirled like brushed hair. As we got to our feet I said idly, 'It looks like a sort of games pitch.'

'Of course, it's for his helicopter. This must be where it lands,' said Joël. I had noticed an orange helicopter above Tréguinec that morning. The chewed-up earth and windswept grass fitted Joël's theory.

'Let's go,' said Mic, 'I'm cold.'

'He must be rich,' I said, 'if he owns a boat as well as a helicopter.'

'He is. He might well be a smuggler,' said Joël. 'This coast has always been full of smugglers. Perhaps that's where his money comes from.'

'For goodness' sake, *come* on,' said Mic. As we turned to follow her Joël said,

'Your hand's bleeding.'

'So it is. I must have cut it.' I held up my hand, and he wrapped his handkerchief round the cut. We walked side by side in friendly silence, while Mic stalked ahead. The clouds had covered the moon entirely; it looked as if the weather was going to break. We said goodnight to Joël, crept to our beds, and in the morning it was raining.

3

We had breakfast inside for the first time since my arrival, and the rain made the dining-room seem pokey and dark. Patrice and Etienne squabbled and whined throughout breakfast, and were clouted by Madame who was exceptionally bad-tempered that morning. I saw her take two aspirins and rub her forehead with her hand. Her headache was going to get no better with the boys yelling indoors all morning. Tréguinec on a rainy day was a gloomy prospect altogether.

'You,' said Monsieur, taking Mic by one ear, 'will do some holiday work.' He looked more closely at her, and then at me. 'You both look worn out.'

'We talked till very late.' Mic started up the stairs. I hid my hands in the pockets of my jeans and followed her. While she worked I lay on my bed and tried to read *Le Grand Meaulnes,* which Joël had lent me. It was hard going because I had to look up so many words, and after an hour I got fed up.

Mic threw down her pen. 'Let's go and play ping-pong.'

'What about your work?'

'Oh, pouf!'

'Won't your father really get mad if you don't do it this time?'

'I'll do half an hour and finish the essay.' She did, and worked quickly now the end was in view.

When we got down to Jean's café we found that everyone had had the same idea. Crowds of people were waiting to play, and we obviously wouldn't get the table before lunch. The café smelt of wet clothes and wet skin; the smell of salt was even stronger. One group were sucking aniseed sweets and the café reeked of them. Mic and I shared Jean's smallest ice-cream and talked to him instead of joining the ping-pong queue.

'Who are all these people?' asked Mic as if they had no right to exist.

'They're the crowd who sit at the far end of the beach. Mostly from Rennes,' said Jean. 'But if you come down straight after lunch I'll keep the table for you.'

'I hate the smell of aniseed,' growled Mic.

'How did your party go last night?'

'How did you know we had a party?'

'Heard the noise.'

'Go on. It wasn't that sort of party.'

'Actually, Antoine came in for a coffee earlier, and told me. He said he had a hangover.'

'What's a hangover like?' I asked.

'A real hangover is a bad experience. Your head spins and you feel you want to die. Every movement causes hammers to beat in your brain.' He spoke with feeling.

'If it's so unpleasant why on earth do people drink so much then?'

'Why indeed. It's often a mixture that's fatal.'

'You'd be out of a job if they didn't,' said Mic.

'Too true.' With one winked eye on us, he poured himself a bright green drink, and added water so that it went cloudy.

'What a pretty colour,' I said.

'Nice taste too,' said Jean. He let me sip a little.

'Ugh. How revolting!'

'Ah, to me it's delicious. That's why adults drink too much, it's delicious. The effect only hits you when it's too late.'

'Adults are mad,' said Mic.

'You'll be one yourself before you know where you are.'

'I won't make stupid mistakes when I am.'

Jean threw back his head and roared with laughter. His mouth was full of gold teeth. 'You'll see, Marie-Claire Menard, you'll see.'

'Pouf.' I looked at Mic, at her tough attractive face with its big mouth, at her curly black hair cut short. Her eyes were blue and often cold. She probably wouldn't make a lot of mistakes, she was too selfish. But others would make them on her behalf, I felt sure. She used people; she used me.

'Buy us a Pschitt-Orange,' said Mic. 'It's your turn.' It wasn't, but I couldn't be bothered to argue.

'You must be firm with Mic,' said Jean, as he took the tops off our drinks. 'Otherwise it will always be your turn.'

'What do you mean?' snapped Mic.

'Well, shall we say, you sometimes forget to pay your share.' Then he added something too quickly for me to catch. Mic shrugged angrily, and took her drink off to a table near the ping-pong game.

Jean smiled at me. 'Mic may be bad-tempered and selfish and rude, but she has many good qualities you know.'

'I know.'

'I'm very fond of her. I've known her all her life.' He stared across the room at Mic reflectively. 'She's the most interesting of the Menard children. And she will be the most unhappy.' He muttered the last remark to himself more or less. There was a pause.

'You've worked in Tréguinec a long time then, if you've known Mic all her life.'

'Twenty-one years. I've worked here since I was a boy. My first job was serving in the chemist's shop next door; my second job was helping in this bar. And here I am still, every summer.'

'And in the winter?'

'I work as a waiter in Rennes. My wife and daughter live there, you see. I have a flat there. In the summer I like to be near the beach, the good air.' He stared out towards the rainy beach. 'I'm not an ambitious man. I like simple things, a simple life.' He smiled his lovely kind smile. He talked to young people as equals; his manner never changed for anyone, whatever age.

'I think I probably am ambitious,' I said slowly. The thought of Jean's life, so circumscribed, made me sad. Not sad for him, because he was clearly a happy man, but sad about the whole idea of never changing a way of life, never moving from a small corner of France.

'And what are you ambitious to be?'

I felt myself blushing, as I always did when people asked me that. Jean saw my face and patted my arm. 'Don't tell me if it's a secret.'

'It isn't really, it's just that I never talk about it.'

'That's a secret, then.'

'I suppose it is. Well, I want to be an actress.' There, the words were out, floating in the air; and although *actrice* sounded better than actress, I still felt a fool, not because it was a stupid thing to want to be, but because so many girls said they wanted to be an actress, in the same casual tone of voice they used next day to say perhaps they'd be a vet, the stage was too risky. I was stage-struck; all my deepest dreams were tied up in the idea of acting, and I didn't want to cheapen my future by talking about it.

'Ah.' Jean looked carefully at me. He did not make the usual remarks people make about the stage, the hard life, the insecurity and all that. He continued to examine my face, and finally he said, 'Me, I'm a simple man and I know nothing about the theatre.

But I would say you had a very good face for an actress.'

I wanted to hug him. 'Why? Why do you say that?' I wanted his opinion as much as if he was a world-famous critic. More.

'Your face is not too remarkable, not too strong.' I stared wordlessly at him. 'It is an interesting face because if you change your hairstyle, for example, you look quite different. I think you could play many parts and be a new person for each. Now someone like La Bardot, for example, she's good but she's always the same. That's her strength.'

'Films are different,' I said; but he couldn't have pleased me more.

When I went back to the cottages later, Mic had disappeared. No one knew where she was, and she didn't turn up for lunch. All Madame said, after she had angrily shared Mic's steak between Patrice and Etienne, was, 'She'll get soaked in this weather, if she's doing a soul-search on the cliffs.'

'Serve her right,' said Monsieur mildly. 'Patrice, your manners bring to mind a prehistoric man.'

I wondered where Mic could be, because she wasn't the sort of girl to go wandering about the cliffs in the rain, and she liked her food too much to miss a meal. An hour or so after lunch she turned up looking pleased with herself. She found me lying on my bed, battling with *Le Grand Meaulnes*.

'*Ciao,*' she said smugly, and stretched in front of the mirror. She waited for me to ask where she'd been, and I waited for her to tell me. The silence lengthened. Eventually Mic said, 'I had a huge juicy steak for my lunch.'

'So did we.' Ours had been neither large nor juicy but I wasn't going to elaborate. Mic looked annoyed.

'Antoine cooked me my steak himself.' She watched me closely.

'Antoine? What do you mean?'

'I dropped in to see him and he asked me to

39

lunch.' Her smugness flowed over her like a sticky covering. I longed to hit her. I've never felt such a pang of jealousy in my life, and didn't enjoy the experience. Mic leant close to the mirror and examined a spot on her face.

'Antoine is so nice when he's by himself, he's never sarcastic or rude then. He was charming to me.' She was watching me in the mirror, and I moved out of its range.

Two could play at her game. 'He seems to me rather dull and stuffy. I don't know why you all get so excited about him.'

'Who said we get excited about him? He just happens to be the only presentable man around at the moment.' Her sophisticated manner was aggravating.

'Don't forget he's married.'

She grinned. 'I haven't, but as we were talking it struck me that perhaps he wasn't very happily married. It just struck me . . .'

I was aghast. How could she know this; what made her think he wasn't? All married couples were *married*, and looked much the same to me; being married as such was a state I hadn't given much thought to. People got married and lived happily ever after, as far as I was concerned. My parents are happy together. Or are they? How was I to know? It was disturbing.

'Don't be stupid. How on earth can a girl your age know about things like that?' I had lapsed into English. 'You shouldn't say such things unless you're sure.'

'Oh, tut, tut. I *am* a wicked girl.' Mic minced round the room, shaking her finger. After a pause I said, 'Well, *what* things made you think his marriage was unhappy? Go on, tell me. I don't believe you know.'

'He talks very casually about Marie, as if she isn't important to him.' She looked at me defensively. 'He said Marie has never learnt to cook a steak as he likes it, she doesn't bother.'

'Often the more I care about something, the more casual I am.' I surprised myself by the truth of this, and I think I surprised Mic too. She shrugged.

'Well, anyway, I had a marvellous time there. Better than being at home with my annoying family.' She went off downstairs, and I heard her arguing with Gervaise. She wanted to bring the record-player upstairs; he was using it.

'It's *my* record-player.'

'Fiche le camp!' Gervaise yelled at her. The argument got heated. I decided rainy days at Tréguinec were awful, and hoped there wouldn't be too many of them. I heard Madame wade into the fight. After a while Mic appeared with her record-player, her face red and triumphant.

'I want to listen to Sibelius. Gervaise can lump it.'

Mic was mad about Sibelius, and played her records of his first and second symphonies often. She was very superior when she learned I had never heard of him; my parents took us both to a Prom concert of Sibelius music just before we left for France, and that was the high spot of Mic's stay in London with us. She sat looking rapt, and hummed bits in the interval. I hardly know any classical music, and certainly none well enough to hum it. I'm not sure whether Mic indulges her enthusiasms because she is truly enthusiastic, or because she knows it makes a good impression. Most likely a bit of both.

Mic put her record on, and sat with her feet up on the window sill, listening. 'Hateful rain, I detest it,' she said at intervals, staring at the wet grey world outside. When the record came to an end she said off-handedly, 'Oh, by the way, downstairs there's a record Antoine sent for you. He said he forgot to leave it last night.'

'Oh, thanks.' I was equally off-hand. But I was gratified Antoine had remembered, and went downstairs to fetch the Jacques Brel record, which Mic had left still in its *Au Printemps* bag underneath the coat-

41

rack. Her wet mac had dripped and soaked a corner of the record. I hoped it wasn't damaged, and wiped it on my jersey as I went back upstairs.

That was how I got to know the French song called *Ne me quitte pas,* which I played throughout that summer, and could never have enough of. *Ne me quitte pas* is Tréguinec, is my first experience of love, is that summer of my sixteenth year, and I've no doubt when I'm thirty it will all come back just as clearly when I hear that song. We sat in Mic's room playing the record the whole of that warm stuffy rainy afternoon; we put the song on again and again, until Mic's room became a magic outpost cut off from the world.

'Are you nervous when you think of the future?'

'No, I don't think about it.' Mic always maintained she was a 'realist'. 'What's the point, your life will never be as good as your dreams.'

'Perhaps it will be better.'

'It's pointless to speculate.'

We sat in silence for a while.

'Jean thinks you will be unhappy.' As soon as I'd said this I regretted it. Mic stared at me in silence, her eyes slowly changing in expression; they looked almost frightened when she suddenly flung herself back on her bed.

'When did he say that?'

'Oh, I don't know, today some time, but I don't think he was serious.'

'No, I'm sure he was serious. Otherwise why would he make a remark like that. Perhaps I will be unhappy.' She pulled a loose thread out of her bedspread. 'It's awful to think we can't avoid our futures.'

A pit opened before us; there was nothing we could do to stop the approach of adulthood and its unimaginable realities.

'Perhaps we'll both be lucky,' I said. 'Perhaps we'll both lead very happy lives.' I didn't know what I meant by a happy life.

42

'How can we always be happy? We can't possibly be happy all the time for sixty or seventy years. I'm not even happy now for more than five minutes a day.' Mic suddenly dropped her serious tone. 'Anyway I don't want to be happy all the time, it would be too boring. And it's none of Jean's business to speculate about my future.'

'He wasn't speculating. He said it as if he knew.'

'I expect he's right. I have a devil in me.' She jumped up. 'Life, I embrace you, whatever horrors you hold.' She danced dramatically round the room. 'Let's go and play ping-pong.'

'Don't tell Jean I told you what he said.' I was embarrassed by the likely possibility of her doing this. She gave me an odd look.

'All right. Then you don't tell my mother where I had lunch.'

But Madame, wise to her daughter, did not ask. Instead she told us to go up to Tréguinec village, half a mile inland, and fetch some shopping for her. Mic started to object, then capitulated. We took a large basket and walked along a narrow twisting lane. The rain had stopped and the sky was more blue than cloudy now. The wet tarmac shone, and the trees and brambles dripped noisily. All the sweet smells of a country lane were doubled as the sun dried the rain; I walked along like a dog, sniffing the air.

'You are a stupid romantic,' said Mic, slashing at the cow parsley with the shopping basket.

'Lovely smells after rain.' I over-acted my enjoyment.

'I only like mountains and cities. Brittany is boring countryside.'

'It feels very old, all rounded. I like it.'

'Mountains feel older.'

'No, they don't. Not that I know any mountain scenery well, but I like the sort of countryside where man has lived for a long time. I want to see all those old dolmens near Tréguinec.'

'They're just boring old stones on top of each other. Old tombs.'

'I don't care. I'm interested in them.'

Tréguinec village consisted of a row of shabby shops, most of them part of old stone houses. There was one smart new shop, a clothes boutique aimed at the summer inhabitants. Mic and I glued our noses to the window. Besides the usual trousers and T-shirts, there was a red-and-white striped cotton jacket with matching trousers. I gazed at this outfit: I wanted it desperately, it was so chic.

'Let's go and try it on,' said Mic.

'I've no money.'

'It doesn't matter. We can still try it on pretending we might buy it.' She opened the door and dragged me in. The shop was run by a smart woman who looked at us with a decided lack of enthusiasm.

'We'd like to try on that suit in the window,' said Mic airily. The woman looked even more suspicious of us.

'I'll have to get it out of the window. It's the last one.' She did not move.

'The last one,' said Mic unctuously. 'Well, I do so hope it fits you, Mary.'

The trouble was, it did. I didn't recognize myself in it; I was transformed, slim and smart. I realized why rich women always looked so good; they could afford to buy only what suited them perfectly. Until I came to France I never really believed clothes could make any difference; I thought if one was fat and ugly one would just have to lump it. The French showed me that no woman need look ugly if she is clever at hiding and making the best of that ugliness.

I stood there, looking at myself, with nothing to say. Mic prowled round me, admiring me. She was enjoying herself, acting the advisory friend. The charade went on until I asked how much the suit cost. Even Mic's nonchalance collapsed a little when she heard the price; as for me, I started to take the suit off with such speed that the woman said sharply, 'Be careful, you'll tear it.' She looked very cross with us, and I couldn't wait to leave the shop. As we left Mic stopped and pointed to a row of scarves, and just to annoy the woman began to admire them in English.

'Look, Mary, aren't they pretty?' I edged out of the door as the woman closed in behind Mic. But nothing really put Mic out; she smiled sweetly at the woman, and said, 'Such a nice shop,' before she left at her own speed.

We had to hurry now, to get the food back to Madame in time for her to prepare it for supper. We carried the heavy basket between us down the lane. My head was filled with that delightful suit; I couldn't get it out of my mind, and the more I thought about it, the more the price seemed fair. I passionately wanted to buy it. I schemed over how to get enough money together; if I used all my holiday allowance, I would still need more from my father to make up the price. He would think it ridiculously extravagant. It was silly, I must forget the suit and be sensible. Realistic, like Mic. But oh, how I wanted that suit. I know it sounds a stupid thing to say, but I felt it could change my life. And in London it would be unique. I dreamed about the suit all through supper, and all evening, and at last I decided I would write to my father and ask straight out for the money. He could only refuse, and it might be sold anyway by the time he replied. I wrote a long letter to my parents and went out, late though it was, and posted it before I could change my mind.

4

Next day was cloudy and cool; I was sitting on the beach reading when Mic said, 'Ohh, la-la! Take a look at this, Mary. What elegance.'

There stood Françoise, in my suit. It looked marvellous, even better on her than it did on me. Of course.

Françoise giggled. 'I couldn't resist wearing it. Isn't it gorgeous?'

'Yes.' My voice sounded hoarse, and I wanted to hit Françoise; Françoise who always looked good in anything, and who so unfairly was wearing the first article of clothing I had fallen in love with. I hated her.

'Did you buy it in the dress shop in the village?' asked Mic.

'Yes, just this morning.' So she had taken it, the last one they had.

'Mary tried it on,' Mic said. 'It even looked good on her.'

I could not stand it any longer, so I ran along the beach away from them and up the steep path to the cottages. When I looked round from the top I saw Mic and Françoise staring up at me, talking.

I know it was silly, but I cried over the loss of that suit. It was so enchantingly pretty, it almost had a life of its own.

After a while the silence in the cottage oppressed me; I discovered I didn't want to be alone after all. I just didn't want to see that suit on Françoise, so I went down the road to Jean's café, avoiding sight of the beach.

The café was empty, and Jean was busy writing a letter on the zinc bar top, using that finely squared paper the French always have for schoolwork. His handwriting was large, and he wrote awkwardly.

'One minute, I'll finish this letter.' I watched him sign Jean with a large number of twirls all round it.

'We play ping-pong?'

'O.K., Jean.'

We warmed up for a few minutes, the clatter of the ball sounding very loud in the empty café.

'What's the matter?' said Jean. 'You look very glum this morning. Has Mic been unpleasant to you?'

'No. It's nothing.'

'It's nothing. *Mon dieu!* Every young person says it's nothing, it's nothing even if their hearts are breaking. It's nothing!' He mimicked an imaginary girl, making me laugh. 'That's better. Now, tell me. What makes you look so sad?'

I nearly said, 'It's nothing' again, because it was nothing really, to be upset that I had lost the opportunity to buy some clothes I liked. 'It's stupid, but I'd decided to buy something I really wanted, and I've just seen someone else wearing it, so I've lost my chance. It was the last one, you see.'

'Pity. What was the something?'

'A suit—a jacket with trousers to match. Very pretty.' I felt a dart of jealousy, and bashed the ping-pong ball as hard as I could. Jean retrieved it from a far corner.

We played for a while, and then I said idly, 'The jacket was red-and-white stripes. The trousers mostly red.'

'Ah.' Jean stopped his serve, and looked up. 'Then

48

it's Françoise de la Tour who has bought them. I saw her just now, looking very smart. I'm right?'

'Yes, you're right.'

'That girl has far too many clothes. Always in something new. It's too much for a girl of her age.'

'She's beautiful, she's lucky.'

'Beautiful? No, she's not beautiful . . .'

'Oh, go on, Jean.'

'No, not to me. Too cold. Narcissistic, selfish. You can see it in her eyes all the time. *Voilà*, that's my opinion.'

I looked at him astonished. Françoise was the height of attractiveness, I thought. I was sure everyone would agree with me, and could hardly believe Jean was serious.

'You're more attractive than Françoise.'

'No, that's nonsense, Jean. I don't believe you. Yesterday you said I'd make a good actress because my face was nothing special.'

'You're twisting my words—I said you had a *flexible* face; that's quite different.' He did a paster of a service, so quick I couldn't see it. 'That will teach you to underrate yourself.' We played intently for a while, but I will confess his remarks cheered me up. When we had finished our game, I bought a Pschitt-Orange and drank it slowly, sitting at the bar on a high stool. Jean counted small piles of change, whistling through his teeth.

'I'm off, Jean, to have a swim.'

I waved my fingers at him, and left.

The weather turned fine and Monsieur Menard decided to take us all on a walking expedition to Ploumanach. He said to me, 'Ploumanach is extraordinary. Huge red rocks, unforgettable. You mustn't miss it.'

In the end a fairly large group set off, Monsieur, Antoine, Joël, Mic, Angélique, Gervaise and myself. We took the inland path until we had skirted the Baron's property. I heard Monsieur say to Antoine,

'Strange man, that. Never takes any part in local life. Never see him, yet he's here all the time, they say.'

'Yes, he's strange. I went to his house once for dinner.' I started to edge up behind them as close as I could. 'He has a very nice house there.'

'I didn't know you knew him.'

'I don't, Marie knows his wife. Or rather, ex-wife, because apparently they're separated now. He . . .' He looked round, saw me behind them, and did not go on with what he was saying until he and Monsieur had moved out of earshot. It was clear Antoine considered me still a child, from the way he had looked at me before going on. It was hurtful, because I'm sure I know enough about things not to be surprised or shocked.

I walked by myself until Joël came alongside. He often made a point of being near me and talking to me; he obviously liked me. He was easy to talk to, and had unusual opinions which he had thought out for himself. He was shy and gangly, but underneath this he had a strong character which sometimes burst out untidily. He grew on you.

After walking for ages, we saw the Ploumanach headland about a mile away. It was indeed spectacular, huge rounded red rocks piled like a giant's game of bricks. We all quickened our pace, and that was when my foot disappeared into a rabbit hole and I twisted my ankle. It hurt so much I could hardly walk on it, and after a while I realized my part in this expedition was over. My ankle was agony, and I couldn't go on. When I said this everyone started to fuss around me, concerned or fed up. I sat down on the path.

'And we're nearly there,' said Mic, one of the fed-up brigade. Her father quelled her with a glare, and said kindly to me, 'We'll get you to Ploumanach, and you can go back by bus. Put one arm round my neck, and one round Antoine's, and we'll make progress that way.'

Antoine helped me to my feet again, Joël took my things, and off we went. Being so close to Antoine made me forget the pain in my ankle for a while. His skin
50

was very warm and smelled faintly of something nice. I noticed a silver chain, bright on his brown wrist; black hairs tangled in the links.

'How's it going?' he said, after we'd hobbled along for ten minutes or so.

'Not bad.' In fact I knew I was in for hours of pain, but I didn't want to alter my method of progress.

Monsieur Menard altered it for me. We passed a path leading to a small granite cottage, and he stopped and looked closely at my face.

'It's hurting you a lot, you look pale.'

'Yes, it is.' Despite myself, I could feel tears rising.

'Right, we'll go in here, and leave you if it's possible, while an advance party goes to Ploumanach to fetch some sort of transport.'

By this time there was nothing I wanted more than to sit down and soak my ankle in hot water, which always eased it.

We entered the tiny two-room cottage through a yard full of chickens. The solid Breton woman who came to the door looked in suspicious silence at Monsieur, Antoine and myself. At the gate the others waited impatiently.

Monsieur explained what had happened and the old woman let us unwillingly into the kitchen. She and her husband were eating their midday meal; she made me sit down at the table in her chair. She asked me something, but I couldn't follow her rich Breton accent. Monsieur translated for me, and a bowl of hot water was prepared.

The old man went on eating his food while he watched us. Their meal was simply green haricot beans and bread, but it looked very good. He broke off another piece of bread, and pushed beans on to his fork with it.

Monsieur and Antoine talked quickly together, discussing what was to be done. I followed some of it, and guessed I was to be left at the cottage while they all went off to Ploumanach. The thought of being left with

51

two old Bretons whose dialect I couldn't understand was depressing. My ankle was now hurting so much I wanted to moan.

'Goodbye,' said Monsieur. 'We'll be as quick as we can.' He and Antoine left the cottage, and the old woman smiled and nodded encouragingly at me. The old man drank some cider and sucked his teeth. Then I heard footsteps and Antoine came in again carrying part of the picnic. I don't think I've ever felt such a flood of relief and pleasure, because he was clearly going to stay and keep me company. He explained to the old woman that we would eat our picnic outside, so as not to bother them. The old woman thought we were mad, and insisted on clearing a place for us at the kitchen table. Throughout all this the old man went on methodically eating his food, breaking off bread and pushing tender green beans on to his fork with it. There was a heavy smell of garlic from the pot of beans. The old woman offered us some and because Antoine refused, I did. It was silly of me, because I longed to taste their simple food.

Antoine talked stiffly to the old Bretons; he obviously felt as shy as they did. To our mutual relief he helped me hobble outside as soon as the meal was over. My ankle was so swollen it looked as if I had developed a growth. We sat down on a stone wall in the sun. Antoine fetched a bucket, and lifted my foot on to it; this eased the pain considerably.

'It's now two o'clock,' he said. 'I should guess Philippe will be back here by three, particularly if he leaves the children to amuse themselves in Ploumanach. He's planning to find a taxi and come here by road to fetch you.'

'I've spoilt the whole expedition.'

Antoine shrugged. 'No one twists their ankle on purpose.' There was a short pause, in which he threw pebbles aimlessly into some nettles.

'I ought to have known better, my ankle is weak and it's always turning over.'

52

'My ankles used to be weak too.' Nothing looked weak about Antoine now. 'Once I remember I twisted my ankle when I was skiing, and I rolled over and down a long slope, with my skis still on. Not only did I spoil that expedition, but I had to spend the rest of my *vacances* sitting around at the hotel, and it was excessively frustrating and tedious.'

I stared at him gloomily. 'I'm going to be stuck for a few days too.'

'At least you can sit on the beach or swim. When you're left alone in a hotel while everyone else is whizzing down slopes having a marvellous time, then it's real hell.'

I could see his point.

'But you know, that miserable week had a good result,' he said reflectively. 'I read one of the few books I found lying about in the hotel, a book about rocks, their formation and substance. It was absorbing, probably because I had nothing else to distract me. That was the beginning of my interest in geology. Now, I'm a geologist, and a lecturer at the Sorbonne. So you see twisted ankles can lead to good things.'

And mine had already, after all; here I was alone with Antoine, cut off from the others for at least another hour.

'And you, do you plan to go to university?'

'My parents want me to go.'

'To Oxford, eh?'

'Well, Cambridge if possible; my father went to Cambridge. But it's very difficult to get in, very very difficult.' I sighed. I wanted to go to Oxbridge because the opportunities to act there were better than elsewhere.

'In France, too many people can go to university. As a result, all the universities are crowded; people can't get in to lectures because the halls are too full. It's depressing. I hardly know any of my students personally now. I like young people, I like to get to know what they think. I'm young myself, after all.'

Something in my face made him laugh. 'But I *am* young, Mary. How old do you think I am?'

I could feel myself blushing all over, down to my swollen ankle.

'I'm thirty-two. That's young for an assistant professor, I can tell you. Most of them are old and out of touch.' He smiled, a smile that always seemed a bit mocking. 'You won't believe me, but I feel younger now than I did ten years ago. When I was twenty-two the world was a very serious place, full of wrongs I was going to put right. Oh, what hard work life was then.' He laughed to himself. 'Desperate, agonizing hard work.'

'Isn't the world a serious place any more?' I wasn't sure what he meant.

He did not answer, but sat thinking, twisting his silver chain round his wrist. After a while he suddenly became aware of me again. 'What did you say? Sorry, I wasn't listening.'

'It doesn't matter.'

'You asked me a question? What was it?'

'Whether you thought the world was still a serious place or not.'

He laughed again. 'Sometimes I think the world is a tragic joke. Sometimes I find it a lovable joke. But no, not very serious. I don't care enough any more, and it's caring that makes life seem serious.' Though he spoke lightly, his words frightened me in a way I find difficult to define.

'Don't you care about anything, then?'

He shrugged. 'I like my work. Geology is my passion, in fact. But politics, religion, morality, etcetera, etcetera . . .' He snapped his fingers slowly. My foot slipped off the bucket and he put it back carefully, having shifted the bucket to make it firmer. As he did so he said, 'But I shouldn't be talking like this. You're too young. You must learn to care before you reject.'

Though I followed his words, I did not see what they meant. We sat in silence as I thought about his

54

remarks; chickens clucked around us. A battered cockerel went strutting past; half his tail feathers were missing, and one of his claws was damaged, so he walked very oddly, stiff-legged. I started to laugh, and when Antoine caught sight of the cockerel he laughed too. The cockerel loped off behind what was probably an outside lavatory.

The old Breton farmer walked past us, ignoring us, and disappeared into a field behind the cottage.

'They are very proud and secret, the Bretons,' said Antoine. 'They mistrust everyone they don't know. Particularly Parisians.' He yawned and stretched. 'It's a wonderful sight when they all get angry with the Government and block the roads with produce. I saw a road outside Quimper filled with mountains of artichokes. Fantastic sight.'

'Why did they do that?'

'Some protest against inadequate subsidies. I don't know. These matters aren't very interesting. But those artichokes were a glorious sight. Surrealist.'

We sat in silence again. Antoine lit a Gauloise reluctantly; it was the last in his packet. He threw the empty packet into the patch of nettles. 'Philippe had better come soon, or I'll die of Gauloise starvation.' He drummed his fingers on his knee while he smoked greedily. After a while I asked him,

'How old were you when you read that first book on geology?'

'What? Which book?'

'The one you just told me about, on the skiing holiday.'

'Oh, yes, that. I suppose about fourteen, perhaps even younger. I don't remember.'

He was bored with me; he got up and strolled off round the cottage, whistling to himself. I sat and stared at the old battered bucket and my swollen foot. There was total silence from the cottage; I expect the old woman was asleep. It was hot and sticky, and the heat brought out the smell of chickens, compost and general dirt.

When Antoine returned it was after three. 'No sign of them,' he said. 'I've been along the road. Perhaps Philippe found it difficult to get a taxi to come here.' He sat down beside me again. 'How I want a fag.' I put my weight on my ankle, to see how it was; agonizing. Antoine sighed. He was hot and bored, and cigaretteless, and it was all my fault. I felt miserable. He would surely avoid me from now on. I began to long for the others to arrive too, because it would stop me from blacking my books even further in Antoine's eyes.

'I really like that Jacques Brel record,' I said. He did not answer.

'Thanks for ruining the day,' said Mic waspishly when I finally reached Ploumanach and the bus home.

The next day all I could do was hobble. I sat in the sand or wallowed in the sea, and got a pleasant amount of extra attention. Even the priest came and gave me his condolences; Jean sent an ice-cream via Joël. There was no sign of Antoine all day.

Mic said she had met an Englishman in Jean's café. It was annoying to find another English person in this small, unremarkable, very French resort.

'He's typically English, he looks a mess,' said Mic with her usual charm and tact.

'Is he staying or just passing through?'

'He said he was here for a few days. I told him I had an English girl staying with me and he looked unenthusiastic.' Clearly the Englishman felt as I did.

'How old is he?'

'Oh, oldish, about Antoine's age.'

'Antoine is young, only thirty-two.'

Mic stared at me. 'How do you know that?'

'He told me yesterday when we were talking.'

'Well, I don't care, thirty-two is old. Twice your age. I call that old.' She flounced off. She retaliated later; she pinned a notice saying *Blessée dans la guerre* on the

56

back of my suit, and I sat all afternoon not knowing it was there. Finally Joël took pity and removed it.

The next day, walking more or less normally, I went to see Jean. Antoine was in the café sitting at a table talking to a strange man. They were laughing and talking so much they didn't see me come in, but Jean gave me a great welcome. He lifted me on to one of the bar stools, and we chatted gaily, but I could feel my eyes swivelling over to Antoine's table. I wondered who his friend was. At that moment Antoine got up with their cups.

'Jean, two more *cafés au lait* please. Ah, Mary! How is your foot? . . . Good, good. One packet of Caporal, Jean, and matches. Oh, and a packet of Gitanes for Pierre.'

Antoine's friend drummed his fingers on the table, frowning vaguely into the distance as he waited. Antoine did not introduce him, and when he returned to the table they resumed their animated conversation. Soon after, they left, still talking.

I wondered whether I would ever, when I was older, have such relationships with my friends, and have so much to talk and laugh about. A soul-mate, so to speak. The two men were not aware of their surroundings at all, they seemed so interested in each other. No wonder Antoine found me boring; I had nothing to say.

'Now, my girl,' said Jean sternly, making me jump. 'It's stupid to think you're in love with Antoine, you'll only get hurt if you let yourself believe things like that.'

I could feel myself blushing bright red. I didn't know what to say. I was appalled to discover my feelings were so obvious.

'I'm not in love with him,' I got out eventually. Jean snorted.

'You've been staring at him like a sick calf ever since you came in here, infatuation on every inch of your face.'

'Oh, God.'

'You must learn to hide your feelings, *ma petite*. Feel

them, but hide them.' He patted my arm. 'No, don't feel them for Antoine, you'd only be miserable. You must save your feelings for someone your own age.'

'I can't help it. I'm a fool. I know Antoine hardly registers my existence.'

Jean sighed. 'Yes, you're a fool. Never mind. We've all got to start falling in love some time.'

'I've never been in love before.'

He laughed. 'I should be surprised if you had. Ah Mary, Mary, you won't forget this summer in Tréguinec! No one ever forgets the first time they lose their heart.'

I felt very pleased I had Jean for an ally. He went on,

'I remember my first love so clearly. I went to stay with an aunt in Nantes, and next door lived a girl called Angèle. She looked like an angel too; long yellow hair and blue eyes, and I fell passionately in love with her. I was about fourteen, I suppose. She was older, about sixteen.'

'Go on.'

'There's nothing to tell. I watched her from a window. I followed her in the streets. She smiled at me occasionally, and I thought I would die of joy.' He chuckled. 'If she'd spoken to me, I think I *would* have died, from fright.'

'Did she know you were in love with her?'

'I don't think so. She hardly noticed me, except as a spotty little boy who stared at her. When I returned to Nantes a year later, my fair Angèle had become an ordinary fat Breton girl, who argued harshly with her mother, and giggled on the pavement with her friends. Very sad.'

'You must have been disappointed.'

'My love died in an instant, like that.' He snapped his fingers. 'And I'll confess I felt a sneaking relief that I didn't have to spend my holiday in agony again.'

'What happened when you next fell in love? Was that agony too?'

'Of course. But luckily one forgets in between how awful it was, like the dentist.'

Going to the dentist didn't seem an apt comparison with my feelings for Antoine, but I saw what he meant.

'Next year, when you come here to stay and see Antoine again, you'll marvel how on earth you fell in love with such an ugly selfish prosy fellow.'

'He's none of those things, Jean . . .'

Jean laughed at me. 'You don't think so now. . . .'

'I'll never think so.' I was about to argue with him, when I saw his expression change; someone had entered the bar behind me. This time I sensed from his expression it was someone unfamiliar.

'Here is the English girl,' said Jean.

I turned and saw a nondescript youngish man, who politely shook my hand, saying as he did so, 'Thomas Sands. How do you do.'

'My name's Mary Meredith.' He had a lopsided smile, and my first instinct was not to like him much. He indicated the bar.

'May I offer you something?'

'No, thanks.' I felt angry at being dragged back into speaking English, and my tongue bunched around the words. 'See you later, Jean. We'll continue our discussion.' As I left I heard Thomas Sands speaking fluent French to Jean. That was the giddy limit. He looked so English I had somehow expected his French to be nonexistent.

I heard someone shouting, '*Attends*, Mary,' and I saw Suzanne Joubert with hundreds of her little brothers and sisters in tow. They were all very brown and scruffy, and the little boys' hair, cut *en brosse*, was always filled with sand. One of them, Dominique, was the most mischievous little monkey I've ever seen—his face was one big grin, and every day he got himself stuck on top of something or tried to drown himself in the sea.

'Dom-Dom, leave that alone,' said Suzanne automatically, when he started rootling in some rubbish at the side of the road.

'But it's . . .'

'Don't pick up dirty bits of paper.'

'But it's money paper,' he said indignantly, and sure enough it was. All French notes are so battered they look like rubbish anyway, and this one was no exception. Dominique's eyes glowed.

'Let's go and buy ice-creams.' So we all flocked back to poor Jean's café, and spent the money on ice-creams for everyone. Thomas Sands watched the invasion from a safe distance.

'Mary, Mary,' shouted Dominique, enjoying himself as he distributed largesse. 'This big one's for you.' He was only five, but he knew what he was up to all the time.

'You seem to be popular,' said Mr Sands to me in English.

'They're my friends.'

'Clearly.'

Dominique looked at him suspiciously and asked me, 'Why is he talking like that? What is it?'

'He's talking English.'

Thomas Sands bent down and said in his perfect French, 'You see, in our country, we all talk this language English. Even little children.' Dominique looked unimpressed, and said, 'Mary talks like us,' before running out of the café. Suzanne rushed after him; he naturally crossed a road without looking for traffic.

I left too, but Thomas Sands followed me. 'You seem to know the ropes here. Have you been here long?'

'Only a week or two. I'm staying with a French family.'

We stood at the top of the beach; I was waiting for him to go away. Sands looked up at the headland.

'I'm told a Baron owns that land.'

'That's right. He's called de la Parmentière.'

Sands repeated the name. As he did so the orange

helicopter buzzed overhead, and disappeared over the headland. The noise stopped, so it must have landed.

'That's his helicopter.'

'I think I'll go and see him,' said Sands suddenly. 'I'll go now. I want his permission to look at a dolmen on his land. Thank you for your information. Goodbye.' He strode off. He had an odd brisk manner of talking and walking.

As I went down on to the beach I met the priest leaving it, followed by his orphans. He smiled, shook my hand, and said he would expect me at three at the orphanage. I had completely forgotten this arrangement, and my heart sank. I sat all the rest of that morning trying to work out what I could talk about.

'You look miserable,' said Joël, sitting beside me. 'What's the matter, bad news from London.'

'No.'

'Good.' He smiled at me. He had a very nice smile. 'Then what is it?'

I explained, and he laughed. 'You should never have agreed. That priest is a dreadful old cadger.'

'It's too late, I'm stuck with it. What, oh what shall I talk to the little devils about?'

'Something that will interest boys.'

I groaned.

'Tell them what it's like living in London. These little boys have never left Brittany. They'll be interested in everything. The metro, the Tower, Buckingham Palace . . .'

His pronunciation made me giggle. 'Our metro is called the Underground, or the Tube.' He repeated the words, and made me laugh again. He enjoyed making people laugh.

'Show things to do with London, if you have any with you. Postcards, snapshots, you know.'

'I didn't bring anything like that with me. Why should I?'

'I bet Mic brought lots back though.'

'Of course. They're all over her table. And come to

think of it, I've some family photographs that would do.' We had taken a river steamer from Putney to Greenwich once, and my father had taken lots of photos of us against the famous river landmarks we passed. For some reason they were all in my writing case. 'I'll go up to the cottage now and sort them out.'

'I'll come too,' said Joël. 'You can try them out first on me.'

'Let's have a swim first.' The tide was high, perfect for bathing. As we climbed the path up to the main road and the Menards' cottages, Antoine and his friend passed us, obviously going for a swim. I didn't want to be caught with Joël, so I forged my way ahead, trying to show that I was on my own, and that Joël had followed me by chance. It was mean, and it embarrasses me even now when I think of it. And it was all to no purpose, because Antoine was busy talking and hardly noticed us.

When we reached the top, Joël said, 'You don't want me with you, do you?'

'Of course I do. Please don't go.' He looked undecided, so I added with truth, 'I need you.'

So we ensconced ourselves in my room, and I showed him the few mementos of London I happened to have with me. One object fascinated him: it was one of those glass paperweights enclosing a snow scene, which had belonged to my mother when she was a child. It was small, beautifully made, and showed the statue of Peter Pan in Kensington Gardens. I usually took it with me when I stayed away from home.

I explained who Peter Pan was and where the statue is to be found. Joël kept shaking the glass ball and watching the flakes swirl.

'You must show them this, they'll love it.'

'It belonged to my mother when she was a child.'

'Did she live in London like you do?'

'No, she lived in Scotland. An aunt of hers sent it to her from London. She says it was the best present she ever had.'

As Joël handed the glass ball back we heard foot-steps clumping up the wooden stairs. He got off my bed and wandered over to the window. Mic came in, and not seeing him at first, said, 'What on earth are you doing here? You'd think it was raining or something.' Then she saw Joël. 'Oho!'

'Shut up.'

'Well, well, well . . .'

'I have to teach the orphans this afternoon and Joël was helping me think up some ideas, if you must know.'

'I bet.'

'You're stupid,' said Joël, and left us quickly.

'What's got into him . . .' Mic was enjoying herself. When I did not reply she went into her room and clattered about.

'If it comes to that, what are *you* doing inside on a day like this?'

'I came to get my knucklebones.' She grinned.

I looked her up and down. 'You're a born trouble-maker.'

'Me. A troublemaker.' She opened her mocking eyes wide.

'You make difficulties between people by implying things that aren't true.'

'I just can't think what you mean.'

'You know exactly what I mean.' Mic hummed to herself while I collected my material together and put the glass weight on top. 'Could I borrow your postcards of London?'

'What for?'

'My talk to the orphans this afternoon.'

'Don't let them get pinched.' She fetched them for me.

We returned to the beach for a final half hour of sun before lunch. Joël had gone, though the rest of the Jouberts were still sitting about.

Little Dominique came and sat on my lap like a trust-ing puppy. Over his bristly sand-filled hair I watched Antoine and his friend walk up and down the sand at

the sea's edge. They were still talking and laughing together. I longed intensely for the time when I would be
adult, would have friends as close and interesting as
Antoine's. But I knew I was still too green to have
friendships of that sort; I had nothing to say, and I was
self-conscious with people I cared about. Oh, the hell
of being fifteen. I imagined myself an attractive intelligent actress; Antoine would find me interesting then.
But in ten years' time he would be over forty, perhaps
fat and bald. I watched him walking in the shallow
sea, gesturing and laughing, his body slim and brown.

5

By the time I reached the orphanage I wanted to be swallowed up by the earth. I saw a row of boys' faces peering over the wall, watching for my arrival; as soon as they saw me they disappeared but I could hear them giggling and whispering. The priest welcomed me with bowings and scrapings, and led me to a bare schoolroom. He rang a heavy noisy bell, and the boys filed in, agog. Thirty beady eyes watched me; if I made a fool of myself they would be well pleased. To get my voice back from its hiding place, I cleared my throat and began to lay out the things I had brought. The boys craned their necks and I passed the stuff round. So, thanks to Joël's good idea, the ice was broken, and the hour passed quite well. In fact, too well, because the priest was delighted and asked me to go again. I hedged a bit, then I had a brainwave.

'There's an Englishman staying in Tréguinec. I'll ask him to do it for you. Then the boys will have a change.' The priest thanked me all the way to the gate in the wall, while the boys crowded behind him chattering busily. I turned and saw the heads again over the wall, watching me go. I waved to them and a dozen hands appeared over the wall and waved back.

On the way to the beach I bumped into Thomas Sands. 'Just the person I was looking for,' I exclaimed. He looked surprised.

'At your service, mademoiselle,' he said. We walked together down the road, and I told him about the orphans.

'It was much easier than I expected. They turned out to be nice boys.'

I'm not worried about the boys. But I may not have very much longer. I've got a lot more places in Brittany to see.'

'Are you just on holiday, or what?'

'I'm writing a book about megaliths. You know, ancient stone monuments. Dolmens, menhirs, alignments —Brittany's full of them, and I need to examine them all if possible.'

'Did you say there was one here?'

'Yes, indeed. There are dolmens all along the coast, but the most interesting is that one on the Baron de la Parmentière's land, and yesterday he refused to give me permission to look at it or photograph it.'

'The mean old man. Well, he isn't old, but he's certainly mean.'

'This Baron doesn't seem to be very popular.'

'Is it surprising? He refuses to let anyone cross his part of the coast; he doesn't let you look at his dolmen. What harm can you do?'

'It's one of the smallest dolmens in existence. I've seen a plan of it in an old book.'

'I tell you what. Next time we trespass on the Baron's land, we'll look out for your dolmen. Then perhaps you could go at night yourself and look at it.'

He laughed. 'Do you make a habit of trespassing?'

'We've been once.'

'It would be useful to know more about the dolmen.' He looked thoughtful. I began to like him.

'If you'll be around for a few days more, will you come and talk to the orphans?'

'Surely.' He gave me a mock-ironic bow and drifted off towards the little hotel he was staying at. I half expected him to turn up in due course on the beach; but there was no sign of him.

I left my cards, photos and paperweight back at the cottage on my way down, and on impulse picked up my camera. As I left Monsieur Menard unwound from a deck chair, waving a letter at me.

'This has just arrived. From your father, I think.'

It was a registered letter full of pound notes and a short letter from my father which said, 'Buy those clothes if you're so set on them. And if they suit you so.' I cursed Françoise again. Perhaps the shop could order another suit for me; I could try. There was no bank in Tréguinec, but Jean had said he could change money for us. I rushed straight down to the café. Joël was there playing ping-pong with Jean.

'How did it go at the orphanage?' Joël asked eagerly.

'Fine. Absolutely fine.'

'Clever girl.'

'Game set and match,' said Jean. He handed me the bat. 'You play now.'

'No thanks, I'm dying for a swim. I just wondered whether you could get some money changed for me.' I waved the pound notes at Jean. He pretended to goggle.

'It's a fortune.'

'My father sent me the money to buy that suit. Isn't it maddening that Françoise got there first. But anyway I'm going to try to order another.' I hadn't much hope; the boutique was not the sort that would repeat things.

Jean counted the notes, and stowed them carefully inside his *carte d'identité*. 'I'll bring you the francs tomorrow. You've got a generous father.'

'Not often, but when he is he does it in style.'

Joël and I hurried off to the beach. It was almost deserted; Joël said that a summer circus had arrived and everyone had gone to watch them settle in. I could see crowds of people at the far end of the village, where there was a flat rough piece of ground, a sort of common.

'Do you want to go and look?' asked Joël.

'I'm too hot.' I dashed into the sea and wallowed

happily. After our swim we lay side by side on our towels drying off.

'Are Mic and Françoise over there?' I asked him. An idea had come to me.

'Don't know.'

'Do you know what would be fun? Let's go to the Baron's place now and take a photograph of the dolmen.'

'Dolmen?' He sat up.

'The Englishman says there's a very fine dolmen on the Baron's land but he won't give permission for anyone to look at it. The Englishman is writing a book about megaliths.'

'Ah.'

The thought of giving Thomas Sands a handful of photographs of the forbidden dolmen really pleased me. I would do it very coolly.

Joël leapt to his feet. '*Allons!* Before Mic and Françoise return.' And we were off across the rocks in a flash.

We took the ordinary public path inland in order to get to the other side of the property; it was higher, and would give us a good vantage point to search for the dolmen. We had not seen it on the headland we had already explored, and it seemed unlikely we could have missed anything so large. We crept inside the boundary fence, and made our way to a crag which stuck out, overlooking the whole property. The dust stuck to our skins and made my nose tickle.

'The Englishman is going all round Brittany looking at dolmens.'

'Is he *sympathique?*'

'Yes, I think he is.'

'Mic didn't like him.'

'I didn't to start with.'

We climbed up the crag carefully and peered over the top. The house lay below us, much larger in area than it had first seemed. It was built in a square around a central patio; here two people were stretched out in the sun on long red chairs. The one on his stomach looked like the Baron; the other, lying on her back in sunglasses, was a very slim brown woman. A little dog was curled up under her chair, just his tail showing. The woman slapped herself, chasing off a fly. A servant came out with a tray of glasses, and left it beside the woman. She sat up, and we ducked back out of sight while she mixed drinks. When we peeped out she was supine again.

We searched the whole property carefully from our vantage point, but could not see the dolmen anywhere.

'No dolmen,' whispered Joël. 'Your Englishman has got it wrong.'

I took some photographs anyway, to show Thomas Sands he was mistaken. Then we returned to the beach and played cards together.

The following day I nipped down to see Jean early, straight after breakfast. I had made up my mind that if the boutique couldn't get hold of another red-and-white striped jacket and trousers, I would buy something else fetching and French. Jean was busy sweeping out the café, and pushing mounds of sand and bits of shell out of the door with his brush.

'If I left it, by the end of the summer my café would be knee deep in sand.' He leant on his brush and stared at me with a curious expression. 'I haven't got your money.' He shook his head sadly.

I gazed back. 'Couldn't you get it changed?'

'*Mais oui!* I had it changed. But I haven't got the money any more.'

I didn't know what he meant; had he lost it, or borrowed it for his own use? He was behaving very oddly, and refusing to meet my eye. I felt slightly sick; I had trusted him entirely.

He moved to the back of the café and put his broom away. Then he reached for something and brought a roughly wrapped parcel towards me.

'I haven't got the money, but I have got this instead. *Ne t'inquiète pas, ma petite.* Unwrap it and see.'

So I undid the string (saved pieces joined together) and there was my red-and-white suit. On the top, tied up in a polythene bag, was a small amount of French money.

'Your change.'

I grabbed him and hugged him.

'Jean, Jean, you're a genius. Where *did* you get this from?'

'Aha. That would be telling.'

'Tell. Where did you find an identical suit?'

He looked at me as if he was weighing something up. Then he said, 'You'll probably ferret it out anyway, so I might as well tell you. I persuaded Françoise to sell it.'

I gaped at him.

'She wasn't very keen. But since I paid her the full price, she didn't lose by it.'

'Surely she didn't want to part with it . . .'

'No, she didn't. I appealed to her generosity, that's what I did.' He smiled to himself. 'Anyway she has more clothes than she knows what to do with.'

'Oh, Jean.' The suit was mine; I could hardly believe it. 'You're a very kind man.' I was more thrilled with Jean than the suit.

'But I've done nothing, just negotiated.'

'It's the nicest thing anyone has ever done for me. And I don't know how you managed to persuade her.'

'I like the young.' He looked embarrassed. 'I bribed Françoise with a thousand ice-creams.'

'She doesn't eat ice-cream. She wouldn't do a thing like that for something like ice-cream anyway.'

'Look, Mary, you've got the suit, and that's an end to the matter.'

'Sorry.'

He started to wipe the tables down; he did this methodically, three broad sweeps of his wet cloth and no wasted effort. He must have wiped those tables thousands of times. I stroked my new clothes, and watched him.

'You must wear those to the dance here on Friday. Then I'll see them on.'

'Dance?'

'The last Friday in every month during the summer we have a hop here. It's usually good fun. Everybody comes.' He squeezed his wet cloth and hung it out. Attached to the rectangular wooden building at the back was a small lean-to, where Jean had a bed and a few possessions. He slept there during the week, and returned to his family at weekends.

'My wife and daughter are coming to the dance,' he said. 'They always come to the August one because it's the best. I thought Mic would have told you about it, she was discussing it yesterday.'

'Mic never tells anyone anything if she doesn't feel like it.'

Jean laughed. 'Too true. I asked her specially to take a message up to Madame Menard. "No messages today," she says and prances off.' He tidied the stacks of cigarettes, and wiped some of the bottles which had become sticky. There were morning smells and noises all around; a delivery van stopped and honked a French-sounding horn. Jean went out to receive some cartons and chat to the driver. I held my new jacket against myself; it was faintly scented, and there was a smudge of powder on one lapel. I was sure my clothes never smelt so sweetly of me.

Thomas Sands came in and ordered coffee and croissants. He settled himself at a table.

'I took some photographs for you yesterday,' I said after a while. Sands looked up; he had croissant flakes round his mouth.

'Photographs of what?'

'Well, of the Baron's property.' His eyes sharpened. 'We couldn't see the dolmen anywhere. I took the photographs to prove it.'

'When was this?'

'Yesterday afternoon.'

'Have you had them developed?' I shook my head. 'Let me have the roll, and I'll have them done for you.'

'O.K.'

'I can't understand your not seeing it. There's a fine example on his land. It could be overgrown, of course.'

'The Baron's property is not the overgrown sort. I'm sure the dolmen isn't there. Joël and I had a thorough look. And the other night we crept about his property, and never saw it either.'

'You and your friends seem to spend a lot of your time surveying the Baron's land.'

I laughed. 'There's not much else to do.'

Thomas Sands looked through a folder and pulled out a map. It was a photostat copy of an old map, and he had carefully annotated it. 'This is remarkably accurate about the whereabouts of all the megaliths. It hasn't been proved wrong.' He put his finger on Tréguinec. There on the headland between the beach we used and the Baron's private beach, was a little dotted circle. 'Dolmen.'

I was puzzled. 'That's where we explored the other night. There was no sign of a dolmen. I suppose it could have got covered with brambles.' I visualized the headland bit by bit in my mind. 'Perhaps that's why the Baron won't let you in to see it; he can't be bothered to clear it.'

'Could be.' He was unconvinced. 'That dolmen has many aspects of special interest.' He frowned to himself.

'Have you asked Jean whether he knows anything about it?'

'He didn't even know there was one there. The locals seem not to notice them, or care what they are. A dolmen is just a heap of old stones as far as they're concerned.'

'I'll ask the Menards about it. Monsieur will surely know.'

'Please do.'

'Would you like us to go again, say tonight, and have

a really thorough look for you? Now we know from the map where it ought to be, we might have more luck.'

He was pleased. 'I'd be very grateful. I shouldn't be encouraging you to trespass, but it would jeopardize my chances of a legitimate inspection if I trespassed and was caught. As I'm not a practised trespasser like you and your crew, I'm sure I would be caught.'

'We won't say you encouraged us.' I grinned at him, and he grinned back.

'If you solve the mystery for me, I'll give you a special mention in the foreword, "And with many thanks to Mary Meredith, who trespassed for me in the interests of truth".'

'Will you really?'

'It's a promise.'

'Will you also talk to the orphans? I promised the priest I would get you to do it.'

He looked rueful. 'How can I refuse?'

'Well, you can't. And we'll do your exploring tonight, if it's a good clear night.'

'That's a deal. Have a drink.' I did.

Antoine came in; I promptly felt all elbows and knees. He was on his own, and came in yawning. I heard him say to Jean, *'Mon dieu,* I'm tired. Pierre and I talked nearly all night.' He yawned again, hugely, his eyes watering, and leant against the bar.

'Bonjour, Antoine. May I introduce an English friend, Thomas Sands,' I said bravely.

Antoine's face was bored and polite as the two men shook hands. 'Antoine Malmaison. How do you do.' I thought he was going to yawn again. He and Thomas were much the same age, I think; Antoine's elegant compact body made Thomas look like me, all elbows and knees.

'Antoine Malmaison?' repeated Thomas, in his excellent French. 'You're a geologist, aren't you? The same name, at all events. I read an article recently on

73

rock formation in Brittany, by Malmaison. Very interesting. Was it yours?'

'Indeed it was.' Antoine looked astounded. 'I didn't think anyone read that journal. Are you a geologist too?'

'No. But I've a special interest in rock types found in Brittany. I'm an archaeologist. I'm writing a book about megaliths, and I need to know whether they are constructed of local stone or not.'

'My dear fellow, you must come and see my collection of rock samples.' He looked delightedly at Thomas. 'My father and I between us have made a remarkable collection. And my friend Pierre Roux, also a geologist, will be pleased to meet you.'

I felt an absurd pleasure myself that I had introduced these two men, a pleasure that persisted despite the fact they went off together immediately without giving me another thought. Jean winked at me.

'These intellectuals.'

'I'm so envious of people with fascinating things to talk about. It must be lovely.' I sighed.

'*Ma petite,* you've a great deal of interesting things to say already. For your age, you're really quite passable company. So stop complaining.'

'Oh, Jean, I don't know what I'd do without you. You bolster up my ego better than anyone does.'

'Flatterer.' But he was pleased.

'But it's true. If people expect you to be interesting, you are, but if they write you off as a boring fat pimply teenager you become one. To perfection.'

'Don't tell me Antoine has the bad taste to write you off as a boring fat pimply teenager?'

'I bet he does. He never even recognizes my existence.

'Antoine always has a lot on his mind. Sometimes he's so deep in his thoughts he doesn't hear a word I say. He can't help it.'

'Anyway he's so clever I never know what to say to him.'

'Monsieur Sands is clever too, and you were chatting away to him as if you'd known him all your life.'

'He's different. He's English.' We both knew that wasn't the whole reason.

I took my new clothes up to the cottage and hung them up. Mic was supposed to be working, but she wasn't there. Her room looked as if a crowd of puppies had been tearing it to bits. Mic's untidiness has something vicious in it. My mother, not excessively tidy, was driven to despair by the state of the spare room while Mic was in it. When Mic got angry she would give the untidiness a stir, until the chaos was complete. She trampled on layers of clothes, and left every drawer gaping. My mother said it looked as if a psychotic burglar had paid a call. I am only tidy with things I like, books and new clothes.

When I got to the beach I looked for Joël; I wanted to discuss the search for the dolmen with him. There was no time to be wasted, because Thomas Sands wanted to move on. Madame Joubert said that Joël had stayed behind to finish some holiday work. He had the first part of his baccalauréat coming up.

'I won't disturb him then.'

'No, you go up, he'll be finished by now. Take this back for me, will you please. That little monkey Domdom brought it to the beach.' She handed me a model train engine which belonged to Marcel. 'Just give it to Joël and he'll put it back in the right place amongst Marcel's things. Hide it quick.' Marcel was nearby. I wrapped the train up in my towel and went off to find the Jouberts' place. It was a wooden chalet they had built themselves years ago, in a small field tucked away behind some old Breton cottages. It was a curious-looking house, so small I wondered how they all fitted in. Joël and Marcel over-flowed into a caravan parked in a corner of the field. I went over and tapped on the window. Joël was writing and looked up, startled. He blushed when he saw me, and pushed back his stool so quickly it collapsed. He grew even more flustered

75

setting it up again. He was doing the most compli-cated-looking mathematics.

'That looks terrifying.' I said. He smiled as he straightened the pages and put them in a folder. The caravan was jammed with boys' things and smelt of glue and socks.

I held out the train, and he groaned. 'Dominique.' He hid the train away in a locker. There was a stiff pause until I said,

'The Englishman wants us to do a job for him. He says there was definitely a dolmen on the Baron's land; he showed me an old map which he says is accurate. He wants us to go and search for it.'

'We didn't see a sign of one.' Joël looked unenthusias-tic.

'I told him that. He wants to know what's happened to it; there was one there, a specially interesting one.'

'I expect the Baron's destroyed it.'

'Could be.'

'Big things to get rid of tidily. There's bound to be evidence of it somewhere.'

'Why should he want to destroy it?'

'He's mad, I expect,' Joël shrugged. 'Aristocrats have to be eccentric to survive.'

'Let's go, just the two of us.'

Joël sat down on his camp stool and fiddled with his biro. 'Mic is bound to want to come.'

'She's bored by old dolmens.'

'True.' He looked quickly at me. 'I'd prefer to go just us. Try and put Mic off.' He was blushing again.

'I'll leave you to your maths. See you.'

I returned to the beach. Mic was lying flat on the sand, her neat body very brown in its pale bikini. I put my foot on her back, and she rolled over quickly, ex-pecting attack. Mic always expected attack; she was usually the attacking party.

'Oh, it's you.' She rolled back again and I lay down beside her. I explained the reasons for the projected

76

search of the Baron's land with as little enthusiasm as possible.

'Would you like to come?'

There was a pause before she said, 'I don't think I'll bother. I've always thought dolmens were a dead bore.' She yawned.

'Don't then.'

'So you and Joël can have a lovely time looking for exciting adventures.'

'Shut up.'

'You'd have thought Joël was old enough to have grown out of these silly expeditions.'

'This is a serious search in the interests of scholarship.' With that I got up and ran into the sea. When I turned I saw Mic sitting up, crossly throwing pebbles into the water.

That evening we all played cards together at the dining-room table; it was hot and still, and moths knocked against the lights. Monsieur Menard was in a particularly good mood and kept us amused all evening. The funnier he was, the crosser Mic looked. When we went up to bed he and Madame were sitting on the window sill, looking out at the sea. He had his arm round her and they looked very content.

Mic went to bed swiftly, ignoring my preparations for the night's jaunt. I was tired now, but I was committed to helping Thomas Sands. Mic made no reply when I said goodbye, though I was sure she was not asleep.

Joël was sitting quietly on a rock, whistling softly to himself. He looked pleased to see me, and we set off at once towards the cliff.

'The helicopter came in early this evening, and hasn't left again. We'll have to be careful.'

'From the map Sands showed me, the dolmen is on this headland, where the helicopter lands.' We searched the headland as systematically as we could, but found no dolmen, or a site that could have once had one.

Then we reached the flat top of the headland, and saw the helicopter like a big insect in the darkness. We crept round it. The pitch it stood on had been specially levelled for the purpose. At one end of the field, half covered by brambles, was a large rough grey stone lying on its side. I grabbed Joël's hand and pointed; we hurried up to inspect it.

'Do you know,' I whispered slowly, 'I think that stone was part of the dolmen.' I realized Joël's hand was still in mine, and let it go.

'The Baron destroyed it to make a landing space for his helicopter.'

The poor stone lay like a small elephant and beyond it in the undergrowth there were no doubt the other stones which had made up the dolmen. We both turned to look at the helicopter on its flat piece of ground, and I became angry at the price the Baron had paid for his convenience. The destruction of something so ancient invited retribution. The air was suddenly full of menace.

'Let's go. We know the facts now.' We aimed for the unmade road which had taken us back to Tréguinec once before. As we turned on to it a voice said,

'And what have we here?' We froze. There was the Baron smiling at us, his hands in his pockets. I grabbed Joël's arm for support.

'We lost our way,' said Joël. 'I'm sorry, is this your land?' I admired his courage, speaking so naturally. The Baron took no notice of him, but stared at me.

'Ah. The English girl who makes a habit of trespass.' He switched from French into English. 'You know perfectly well this is my land. In fact, you seem to have a certain affection for my property.'

Joël looked bewildered at the change in language.

I spoke in English too. 'My friend is crazy about helicopters so we stopped to have a look at yours.'

'Really.' He lit a cigarette, his lighter throwing up a large flame. 'I should have thought it was too dark to see anything much.'

Joël's frustration at being unable to follow the conversation was evident. I was about to apologize and try and leave then and there, when the Baron said roughly,

'Come off it, you didn't come here to look at my helicopter. You're both too old for curiosity of that kind.' He swung round on Joël and said in French, in an accusing tone, 'You didn't come here to look at my helicopter, did you?'

'No, no,' said Joël, falling into the trap.

'That's what your English friend said you had come for.' Joël was silent.

'Now,' said the Baron in a conversational manner, 'while I see you off my premises, perhaps you will tell me the real reason for your visit.' He indicated the road with an ironic gesture, and the three of us started walking down it.

'We wanted to find your dolmen,' I said, in French.

'Ah, my dolmen?' He waited.

'I've seen a map showing it,' I said defensively. 'I'm interested in dolmens.'

'Really. An unusual interest for a young girl.'

'She's very clever, she has all sorts of unusual interests,' said Joël.

'I did not doubt you. Well, did you find your dolmen? I mean, my dolmen?'

'Of course not. It cannot be found, because you've destroyed it.'

'Now, whatever makes you think that?' The conversational manner acquired an edge.

'You made a helicopter landing pitch out of the site where the dolmen once stood.'

We were nearly at the end of the road; the gate was about fifty feet away. The Baron stopped walking, and I stared with longing at that gate, willing myself through it.

'What I did with the dolmen is entirely my own business. It was my property. I have a distaste for dank old objects representing tedious prehistoric religious cults. Now go, both of you, and if I catch you on my land again you will be in serious trouble.' He stood there while we walked away from him. My back itched and I longed to run for it, but Joël kept up an even pace, opened the gate with controlled movements, and said, *'Bonsoir, Monsieur le baron,'* politely as if we had just paid a social visit. He got no reply.

As soon as we were round the first corner we held hands and ran like mad. Neither of us felt like returning to our respective beds until we had calmed down, so we sat in a sheltered corner near the Menards' and discussed what had happened.

'In England, if someone destroyed an ancient monument they could be prosecuted. What's the law in France?'

Joël had no idea. 'I hope he is prosecuted. He is a horrid, cold, selfish man.'

We sat in silence for a while. Then I became intensely aware of Joël's physical presence because he was aware of me. We both inspected our shoes and the ground.

'I hope you're not going back to England soon,' said Joël at last.

'I haven't fixed the date yet.' I tried to speak casually.

'We're all staying for two more weeks.'

'I expect I'll go back before then.'

'Stay as long as you can. Please.'

I got to my feet. 'It's time we went to bed. It must be at least two o'clock. I said I'd teach the orphans again tomorrow.' We walked in silence to the Menards' gate, awkward with each other. As I turned in at the gate he put out his hand and touched my arm. I felt torn in two; drawn to him, yet unwillingly.

"I'll come and meet you at the orphanage. When will you finish?'

'About noon. I start at eleven.'

'I'll wait outside at twelve then. *A bientôt.'*

He walked away, and I heard stones spurt as he

broke into a run. It was nearly three o'clock, I saw from the clock in the dining-room. Mic was fast asleep, calm and angelic in expression; her eyelids flickered and her lips twitched slightly. I dropped into bed and tried unsuccessfully to sort out my feelings about Joël.

Joël met me as promised.

'Let's go and find Thomas Sands and tell him about last night.' He knew where Thomas was staying, but when we got there the proprietor of the little hotel said Thomas had left that morning with all his baggage.

'Monsieur Malmaison drove him away in his car,' he said.

'I bet he's gone to stay at Antoine's. Let's go and see.'

'Why do you think he might be at Antoine's?' Joël sounded unwilling to accept this; he clearly did not much want to go to Antoine's. We walked down the inland road which led to the farmhouse.

'Well, I introduced them yesterday and they went off together talking about rocks, so it's a possibility.' It was a good excuse, too. Thomas being there would give me more confidence. As we reached the gate of the drive, Antoine's Renault came lurching out. He had Thomas and Pierre inside with him; he jammed on his brakes so that they both lurched forward.

'Madman,' said Pierre.

'Do you want to come with us?' asked Antoine. He looked happy, and his lively eyes made my heart thump.

'Yes,' I said.

'*I'm just a girl that can't say no,*' sang Thomas. I blushed.

'Where are you going?' I heard Joël ask.

'Off to look at a dolmen at Trégastel.'

He looked unenthusiastic, but I pushed him towards the car. 'Come on, Joël.' So the two of us squashed into the back of the Renault with Pierre. I had to sit on Joël's lap.

81

'You'll collapse under my weight.' He laughed, looking pink under his freckles. He put one hand tentatively against my waist to steady me. This irritated me; Joël always got on my nerves when Antoine was around.

It was an uncomfortable drive; Joël's knees were bony, and the Renault bounced us all about. But I didn't mind, because my head was very near Antoine's, and I could smell his hair. It had a faint sweet scent. He, Pierre and Thomas were in high good humour and kept up a stream of witty conversation which I just sat and enjoyed. As we swung round a sharp corner Joël put both his arms round my waist and kept them there. I saw a reflection of his face in the driving mirror; he was happy, and not listening to a word of the conversation round him. He only joined in when Thomas asked me whether we'd done our search yet.

'We went last night. And we found that the Baron has destroyed the dolmen to make the landing space for his helicopter. We came to find you to tell you.'

Thomas was horrified.

'What's this?' said Antoine, and Thomas quickly explained.

'I don't believe it,' said Antoine. 'These children have got it wrong. It was probably overgrown and they missed it.'

'We definitely did not.' Joël was angry. 'I know what a dolmen looks like.'

'I do beg your pardon.' Antoine glanced at Joël in the driving mirror, and laughed. 'All this trespassing. Tut-tut.'

'We went at the request of Monsieur Sands. We knew exactly where to look, and we found one of the dolmen stones dragged to the side of the field.'

'Then the Baron caught us,' I said.

'Oh, dear.' Thomas was rueful.

'He was very angry in his icy way, beastly in fact. We challenged him about the dolmen, and he admitted

82

he had had it removed. He said he didn't like dank ancient things, and besides, he needed that bit of land for his helicopter. He was cool.'

'*Salaud,*' said Antoine. 'I hate these rich selfish men.'

'He must be a determined man,' said Pierre. 'Removing a dolmen is not something I would undertake lightly.'

'If men without machines could build it, then men with machines could destroy it easily,' said Joël.

'Too true, oh sage.' Antoine deliberately needled Joël. Joël stared out of the car window and said no more. He took his arms from round my waist, and looked sorry he had come.

'Can he be prosecuted?' asked Thomas.

'I'm not certain of the technicalities of the law on ancient monuments,' said Antoine, 'but I'm sure he can.'

'What's the man's name?' asked Pierre.

'Baron Auguste de la Parmentière.'

'The trouble about a man like that is that he has friends in high places. He will simply exert a little pressure on the right people and any prosecution will be dropped.' Pierre sucked his teeth in a characteristic manner. He was a thin bird-like man, with extraordinarily large ears which even in this heat looked cold. 'The system is so corrupt.'

While he and Antoine bewailed corruption, Thomas asked me politely in English, 'He didn't hurt you or frighten you, did he? He sounds an unreliable sort of man.'

'He was very polite, but frightening.'

'What time did all this occur?'

'About two in the morning.'

'Late. Don't go there again, will you.'

'Nothing would make us.'

We arrived at the Trégastel dolmen after about half an hour's drive. It was on common land, and neglected; briars and weeds had grown up the sides of the huge rough stones, and people had used the inside as a lava-

83

tory, which deterred all of us except Thomas from spending much time in there. When I examined the stones from the outside I wondered how the Baron had managed to dispose of so much sheer weight of rock.

Thomas was taking photographs of the dolmen from all angles; he made me pose against the dolmen as a guide to its size. As I stood there, my legs smarting from some nettle stings, I said idly, 'Well, let's hope the Baron had some photos taken as a record before the bulldozers destroyed his dolmen.'

Thomas looked up in surprise. 'Of course. I must ask him. Let's hope he has indeed.' He packed his camera up and I watched his precise hands. 'In any case, I've got the peak of my trip ahead of me. As soon as I've finished there I'm off to Carnac.'

'What's Carnac?'

'It's a place, further south in Brittany. It's the most astounding collection of megaliths in the western world.' His eyes shone with enthusiasm. 'Amazing. Beautiful.'

'I've never even heard of it. What's the name again?'

'Carnac. Carnac, in the Morbihan, beside Locmariaquer. What wonderful old Breton names! I love Brittany, don't you?'

'I hardly know it. But I'm beginning to.'

Antoine came up. 'Come on, you English tourists. We will introduce you to the joys of the best *crêperie* in Brittany.'

'I know the joys, and I'm more than willing,' said Thomas. We piled into the car and drove a short distance to a shabby café. There we ate the most delicious paper-thin pancakes, stuffed and plain; the smell of sweet butter frying always brings the memory back to me. We sat in a row on a stone wall, eating *crêpes* in our fingers, and I thought I had never been happier. The three men were arguing about the dating of the old stone dolmens and menhirs and tumuli, and I gathered they could have been built any time between 3000 B.C. and 1500 B.C. Pierre held to the latter date but the other two thought he was at least one thousand years out. The age of these megaliths made me realize the full enormity of what the Baron had done. He had destroyed an ancient burial chamber and I hoped its ghosts were haunting him.

Madame Menard was annoyed with Antoine for giving me so many pancakes that I could not eat my lunch. Mic scowled when she heard what I'd been up to all morning, and said crossly, 'Why didn't you come and fetch me?'

'There wouldn't have been room in Antoine's Renault. It was an awful squash as it was.'

'Anyway those old dolmens leave me cold. Just a lot of stones piled on top of one another, by a lot of old savages.'

Monsieur Menard raised his eyes from a letter he was reading and said, 'Do not dismiss what you know nothing about, Marie-Claire. Those megaliths were built by a civilization of great interest. They were a sophisticated people; they wore, for example, beads made in Egypt. They also mastered the enormously difficult engineering problems of moving and erecting those huge stones. Dismiss them as boring when you know more about them.' He returned to his letter, which appeared to contain worrying news. That may have accounted for his short temper. When he'd finished reading I asked him, 'Have you been to Carnac?'

'Of course. Anyone who is interested in megaliths must go to Carnac. It's the Mecca of megaliths.'

'I've been to Carnac,' muttered Mic. 'So I know what I'm talking about.'

'Why this sudden interest in megaliths, Mary? I should doubt whether Marie-Claire's enthusiasm could inspire you,' said Monsieur.

I giggled; he had such a droll dry voice. 'There's an Englishman here in Tréguinec who's writing a book about dolmens and things. He makes it sound very interesting.'

'I met an Englishman briefly yesterday, with Antoine . . .'

'That's him. Thomas Sands.'

'I expect he's here in Tréguinec to look at the little dolmen on the headland.'

I stared at him in surprise.

'When I was a boy that dolmen was not fenced off from the public—the former owner did not mind people on his property. I haven't seen the dolmen for years, but we used to play in it a lot in our *vacances*. It was a friendly baby dolmen. Whoever had been buried there was in favour of us, we felt. We imagined it was a boy prince.'

'I've never seen a dolmen on the Baron's land,' announced Mic. 'Which side of his beach is it?'

'You seem to be well acquainted with his property,' said Monsieur smoothly. 'Has he invited you in?'

Mic blushed. 'No. We've been exploring.'

'Trespassing. Be careful; from all I've heard the Baron is not a very choice character. He might take exception to you if he saw you.'

Mic shrugged and said no more. I felt distinctly uncomfortable.

'Monsieur.' My voice came out too loud. 'I'm afraid the dolmen is destroyed. I've been trespassing too, I went there specially with Joël the other night, to see if we could find any trace of the dolmen. Thomas Sands asked us to, because the Baron would not give him permission to see it. The Baron caught us.' Everyone was listening; even Patrice and Etienne stopped bickering. 'We discovered that he had destroyed the dolmen to make a landing space for his helicopter. The Baron admitted he had demolished it.'

Monsieur said nothing. Eventually Madame said, 'It makes you feel like burning his smart new house down in revenge.'

'Poor young prince,' said Monsieur at last. 'I hope his ghost turns nasty on the Baron. He must have used dynamite to destroy that dolmen.'

86

'We must report him,' said Madame. Monsieur did not answer and presently got up to leave the room. As he reached the door he said, 'When something is three thousand years old, you'd think every man would regard it as inviolate.'

'Some people hate old things,' said Mic. But her father was gone. 'Well, they do.' She was defensive, upset.

'You do, at any rate,' said Gervaise.

'I would never destroy them.' We all ate in silence for a while.

Monsieur came back into the room, holding a sheet of old photographs. They showed a group of children playing on, in, and round a small dolmen. One child, standing on top of the dolmen, was grinning down cheekily, looking very like Mic. It was her father. We all craned to see the brownish photographs. Madame laughed.

'Philippe, I've never seen these before.'

'I discovered them in a box full of childish treasures. I haven't seen them myself since the war.' He examined them, smiling.

'Thomas Sands would be very glad to see these,' I said tentatively.

'Tell him to come up any time and have a look.'

'I will.' I picked up the photograph of Monsieur on top of the dolmen. 'Mic, this might be you.'

'I don't see any resemblance,' said Mic haughtily. Monsieur gobbled at her, and she left the room, thumping up the wooden stairs. Monsieur gathered all the photographs together, and put them in an envelope.

'I will make sure that bastard is prosecuted.'

'Philippe, mind your tongue.'

I went upstairs to find Mic. She had the record-player going and was half way through *Ne me quitte pas*.

> *'Moir je t' offrirai*
> *Les perles de pluie*

she sang in her flat voice. She took no notice of me. When the record was finished I went to the wardrobe and opened it; there was my new suit. Mic stared at it and stopped humming. I realized from her expression that Françoise had not told her about the transaction.

'How did you get hold of that?'

'Françoise sold me hers.'

'She never told me about it.'

'Jean persuaded her. I had nothing to do with it. It was all his idea.' I stroked the sleeve.

'I'm surprised she parted with it.'

'So was I. I paid her the full price, though.'

There was a long pause before Mic said rather sourly, 'I must say, you've got your life very well organized all of a sudden.'

'It won't last.'

'Nothing I really want ever happens to me. All the things I look forward to always turn out to be disappointing.'

I examined my suit without replying.

'What the hell anyway. I always want too much.' With a rough gesture that did the record no good, she put it on again. As the sweet sadness of the song filled the room I shut the cupboard door and sat in my favourite place on the window sill. I felt tense, and found myself saying inwardly, 'Keep sweet, life, keep sweet.'

6

The café had been decorated all over with gaudy paper streamers by Jean's wife and daughter. Paper lanterns had been hung outside it, and as we walked down after supper they looked like red, blue and yellow butterflies in the half-dusk. As we watched the eaves lit up with a viciously bright row of coloured bulbs, and the lanterns became blurred shadows, their delicate effect overcome by the harsh light. Music started: bouncing, throbbing, squeezy music, just right for a seaside hop. We were all excited, and ran the rest of the way. As we got to the door of the café, a large man came out in a white shirt and brocade tie; it was Jean, looking strange out of his usual T-shirt. We all piled into the café.

'You look very nice tonight, *ma petite*,' said Jean to me. He presented me to his wife and his daughter Laure. Laure was older than I was, fat, her face red and shiny with embarrassment. She had already sweated so much her dress was wet under the arms. Jean's wife, in contrast, was tiny, with a gentle smile. We all shook hands.

'Jean tells me a lot about you,' said his wife, after a pause.

'He's a good friend to me,' I replied.

'He likes the young.'

I noticed that Laure was not listening, though she

smiled in my direction. Her eyes were flickering over the latest arrivals.

'He helps me understand French life.' It sounded stupid put like that, so I laughed. Madame Dubois and Laure laughed too, and then we stood in silence. Luckily Thomas Sands came up at that moment and rescued me; I'm bad enough at small talk in English.

'I'm off tomorrow,' said Thomas, 'so this is my farewell party.' He bought a bottle of wine. 'We'll bag this table so that Antoine and Pierre and anyone else who wants to can join us.'

He relieved the only doubt in my mind about the evening; Antoine was coming to the dance. I felt extremely happy.

'They weren't going to come,' Thomas went on, 'but I persuaded them. I have a passion for this sort of hop; always much more fun than any other kind of dance.' He poured a glass of wine for me. 'I've enjoyed Tréguinec. If Carnac wasn't luring me on I'd stay here a little longer.' He sat back and drank his wine. 'You're looking very pretty this evening.'

'Thank you . . .' I was just about to expound the virtues of my new French clothes when I stopped myself. Françoise always accepted compliments with a calm pleased smile, saying nothing; I'd be cool too. At that moment I saw Françoise; she was wearing a long black cotton shift with a brown belt, and she looked different from anyone else in the room. And more stunning. I began to see that besides having a good figure and an innate sense of chic, Françoise always knew by instinct what everyone else would be wearing, and chose something different but not out of place. Much thought went into her daily appearance, much more than its simple effectiveness would suggest. More thought than I would ever be prepared to spend on mine. I saw Thomas appraising Françoise; I would introduce them.

Joël arrived and Thomas offered him a drink.

'Thank you both, by the way, for your midnight efforts on my behalf. I'm going to report the Baron to

90

the authorities, and so is Antoine. But I doubt if anything will happen to him.'

'Monsieur Menard is going to take it up too, and since he works for the Government he might have more luck.' I described his rage over the destroyed dolmen in which he had played as a child. 'By the way, he's got some photographs of it, taken before the war.'

'Oh, *marvellous!* Is he here?' Thomas started to look round eagerly.

'Not yet. I think they're dropping in later with Joël's parents.' I didn't feel like discussing dolmens at the dance, so we didn't go on talking.

Joël sat down on the chair next to me. He had something in his hand, which he placed on the table. 'Present for you.' It was a squat little frog made of limpet shells stuck on top of each other with winkles for eyes; he had clearly made it himself and it wore the sweetest surprised-frog expression. I started to laugh at it, delighted with it.

'Joël, you are a dear.'

He grinned, and with a quick awkward gesture put his arm round my shoulders. 'It's called Euclid,' he said, and we both giggled at the frog.

Thomas called out, gesturing at the door, 'Oy Antoine. *Par ici.*' Here were Antoine and Pierre, laughing together. Joël's arm dropped and he muttered something. I thought he was going to leave, and caught his arm. 'Don't go. Thomas wants everyone to join his table.' His green eyes met mine for a moment and he sat down again.

'Antoine makes me sick,' he said quickly.

'Why?'

'He's so damned pleased with himself.' That was true, I admit.

'He's got a lot to be pleased about.' Joël looked annoyed, as I knew he would.

Antoine clicked his heels together and bending over with exaggerated grace, kissed my hand. He did it to Mic and Françoise as well, but it was nice all the same.

91

'Good evening, tomb-hunters,' said Pierre. He was wearing an amazing purple shirt which made him look more like a bird than ever.

For the first time in my life I really enjoyed a party. I knew a lot of people. I felt confident in my clothes; I was just on holiday with other people also on holiday, and the past and the future had no place in our casual happy fun. In London I never danced much at parties, but here I danced all the time, with Joël, with Antoine, with Pierre, with Thomas, with Jean. Most often with Joël, who stuck near me all evening, until Mic came up and said, 'Look at the love-birds. Isn't it sweet.' Joël growled and disappeared for a while.

'We are *not* love-birds,' I said to Mic. 'Damn you.'

'Oh, no. Of course not.' She opened her eyes wide and innocent, and I was trying to think of a retort that would shut her up when I felt my hair being gently pulled from behind.

'Come and dance, English girl.' It was Antoine. He held me tight, and danced a little unsteadily; he had drunk a lot of wine that evening. The music was slow and quiet, and Jean turned the lights out with a great theatrical 'Aha.' There was a happy roar from everyone, and ribald comments flew about. Being so close to Antoine in the half-darkness made me feel giddy. He was humming away to himself, when he wasn't indulging in back-chat with other people. I had never seen him so animated as he was that evening.

Over Antoine's shoulder I saw Joël standing in the café doorway. He was watching me, angry and unhappy. The next time I looked he was gone; I craned over Antoine's shoulder, and could see him nowhere. He must have gone outside.

Antoine dug his chin into my hair.

'Petite Anglaise. Are you as innocent as you look?'

I could feel myself blushing, and did not know what to say; not that Antoine wanted an answer. We were in the darkest corner of the café now, and his back was between me and the other dancers. He bent and kissed me.

It was the first time I had ever felt a man's mouth on mine. In curious detachment, I reflected that Antoine's mouth was like a large limpet trying to stick to mine. After a very short time he took his mouth away.

'Even more innocent than you look.' He rubbed my cheek with his finger, but I got the impression his attention was no longer on me. 'That was the most innocent mouth I've touched for years.' He yawned.

The music ended. Antoine bumbled off to Thomas's table, and I went to the loo, with a desire to be alone. My mouth felt changed, stained; but in the mirror I looked no different. I was puzzled at the oddness of my first kiss, and at the unexpected muscular slippery feeling of a man's mouth. Kissing was obviously an acquired taste—and perhaps an acquired art too. No soaring violins at all. I looked at my reflection for quite a while as I pondered, and when I finally came out of the loo there was an interval on and most people had gone outside to talk and laugh in the warm dark. Feeling still that my lips were advertising their recent experience too clearly, I slipped out of the café and went towards the beach. As I came up to a kiosk I heard Pierre and Antoine talking. They were sitting on a bench on the other side of it. I froze.

'For a self-declared rationalist, you act too often on impulse,' Pierre was saying, while Antoine laughed. 'No, no, it's true.'

'I live in the moment.'

'Yes, but you also *take advantage* of the moment. That student you got into trouble, for example. You should have never begun to live in that moment.'

'She threw herself in my way, repeatedly. She would have died of disappointment if I hadn't had an affair with her.'

'No excuse, Antoine.'

'I like yielding to temptations.'

'You might count the cost occasionally.'

'It would spoil the beauty of it.'

'Beauty. Pah. Our little English girl, for instance. Why on earth did you kiss her? I can't believe you were yielding to an overpowering temptation. She's still a child.'

'I was tempted, actually. Tempted to see if that innocence was real; and it was. Kissing her was like kissing a warm rubber doll. Perfect innocence.'

'Sometimes you make me angry. You've tampered with that innocence—for what gain?'

'I don't kiss for gain, dear Pierre . . .'

'For her loss then.'

'How do you know? You're being an old-fashioned romantic.'

Pierre made an angry grunt, and did not reply.

'Do her good.' Antoine's voice was colder. 'She's been asking for it, staring at me with big sheep eyes.'

'Come off it, Antoine.' I heard a scrunch as if they were getting up. 'You're too drunk to make sense.' Further scrunching, and I realized that they would see me unless I ran like a shaft of light. I fled up the coast road and went down on to the beach out of sight of the café. I couldn't bear to go back to the dance, so I walked up the length of the beach right to the far headland where we did not often go. The tide was low, and the flat wet sand shone in the moonlight; the smooth boulders rising out of the sand looked like the backs of grey beasts. Inside me was a painful red-hot lump which swelled until it overflowed through my eyes, and hot tears ran down my cheeks. It was a strange sort of crying, because I did not sob, just stared straight ahead while the tears rolled.

I walked down to the edge of the sea, and stood in the shallow breaking waves, shoes and all. Small waves licked round the ends of my beautiful new trousers, and air bubbles rose out of my shoes. The water was warm at the edge, almost as warm as the air. I stood stock still for some time, and then I knew what I wanted to do. My strange tears ceased as I took off

94

everything I had on and put them on a large rock, and went into the sea.

My body was overheated from dancing so I gasped when the cold hit my unprotected skin. At least the shock made me forget the painful lump for a few moments. I rubbed my mouth with seawater as if to wash off for ever any mark of Antoine. I swam quite a long way out to sea, and then trod water, staring back at Tréguinec. The lights looked cheerful and enticing, the café was a gaudy ship. The sound of the squeeze-thump music came clearly across the beach; the dancing had started again. I was pleased, for that meant I had the beach to myself.

The sea was indigo and silver, and friendly. I lay on my back and looked up at the stars; there were no clouds and the atmosphere was unusually clear. As I stared at the carpet of silver dots, trying to make out some of the constellations, the sea lapped and rocked me and I felt a cosmic comfort. The sky and sea had been there, looking the same, for those dolmen-builders.

I started to swim lazily back. Being naked in the water gives one's body an indescribable sense of freedom and power. With each stroke I felt the courage to face my hurt increase. The lump was there, but I would cope. Swimming in total contact with the warm night sea gave me a vision of strength which, looking back, has supported me ever since.

Lost in my thoughts, I hadn't heard a voice calling.

'Mary! Mary!' The tone was sharp and desperate. A figure standing near my pile of clothes was staring out to sea. I waved, and made a splash to show my position. The figure came to the edge of the water and waited, motionless. As soon as I was close enough I could see it was Joël. When I could touch down I started to wade in. 'I'm naked,' I shouted at him.

'What?'

'I'm naked.' My shoulders were out of the water now,

95

and from the change in his expression he showed he had understood me.

"I'll fetch you a towel,' he shouted, and ran up the beach. I went and sat on a rock by my clothes, dripping. I drew my knees up close and hugged them. Joël was back very quickly. I saw his espadrilles flashing as he ran down the beach jumping over the grey boulders. Despite the warm night, I had begun to shiver.

Joël did not look shy or embarrassed at my nakedness; he draped his towel round my shoulders, and then sat down nearby while I got dressed. He threw pebbles into the sea as he waited for me. I felt very grateful to him.

'How did you know I was here?'

A pebble dropped with a splash far out before he replied. 'Pierre told me.'

I could feel my painful lump growing again. 'Pierre?'

'I happened to ask if anyone had seen you when he was near me. He said he'd seen you run off down the beach.' There was a pause. 'He said he thought Antoine might have upset you.'

From the way Joël spoke I realized he had not seen Antoine kiss me. I did not want him to know about it, and hoped no one would tell him.

'Yes, he was rude to me. You know how sarcastic he can be. It was stupid of me to get so upset.'

'He makes me sick. He's always so pleased with himself.'

I didn't answer, and finished dressing in silence. I was still shivering.

'I stayed in too long. But it was so lovely in the water.' I rolled Joël's towel into a sausage. He took it from me, and then with an awkward rush of movements put his arms round me and hugged me close.

'When I saw your clothes, I was horrible afraid.'

'Oh, Joël. I only wanted to get away from everyone for a while.'

We stood together in silence, and I found his shoulder very comfortable and comforting. My shivering stopped.

Torches began flashing at the far end of the beach near the café, and I heard my name being shouted. Joël looked up with a jerk.

'It's Monsieur Menard.' He ran ahead of me up the beach shouting. 'She's here, it's all right.' I followed running and leaping into the air in order to warm up.

'Well?' Monsieur looked annoyed when I came up.

'I went for a swim.'

'A very foolish things to do alone at night. Please don't do it again.'

'I'm sorry.' Monsieur grunted and went off up the beach. I felt about ten years old. When we got near Jean's café I said to Joël, 'I think I'll go back to the cottage.'

He looked crestfallen. 'Don't go. Please come and dance.' He smiled his eager shy smile, then his eyes gleamed. 'You mustn't give Antoine the idea that he succeeded in upsetting you. Bad for his ego.' His smile turned into a grin as he watched my face. I said nothing, but gave him my hand, and he led me into the café. At first I didn't look beyond Joël's shoulder, but slowly courage came and I began to look naturally round the room. Everyone was too engrossed in their own fun to have noticed my absence or the reason for it; and as for Antoine, he and Pierre had left the party.

Thomas was dancing with Françoise, and looked as if he was enjoying himself. Françoise was flirting demurely with him, but underneath that cool exterior I got the impression she was distinctly pleased with her new conquest.

'Antoine's gone,' said Joël into my hair. 'So you needn't worry.'

'I know.' Joël looked pleased, and I felt irritated, and cross with myself. The atmosphere between us cooled at once, and I felt even crosser with myself. After the dance Joël led me back to the table.

'Where's Euclid?'

Joël looked under the table. 'Someone must have pinched him.'

'But I loved him, he had such a funny expression. Let's look for him.'

Alas, the remains of Euclid were discovered in a corner. 'I'll make you another,' said Joël. 'A bigger and better frog.'

Monsieur Menard called me, and announced that he was taking us home. He unfastened Mic from her partner and led us out despite our protests. My protests were not heartfelt, though. I was beginning to long for my bed, in order to consider my full evening in peace and privacy.

Mic was still very lively, and climbed into my Breton bed to talk, deaf to my hints that she was not welcome.

'Buzz off, Mic. I'm tired.'

'We *are* cross tonight. I wonder what happened to make us so touchy.' Her hard eyes mocked me; she knew something had happened but did not know what, and was goading me into giving myself away.

'Yes, I wonder.' I pulled my coverlet up to my chin and closed my eyes firmly. Mic went on regardless.

'Moonlight bathing with Joël. I wonder where it will all end?'

I kept my eyes shut and my face flaccid, and was pleased she knew so little.

'Think what you like.' I remembered Joël's worried but relieved eyes when he came back with the towel, and the tact with which he wrapped it round my folded naked body. I knew that for his age Joël was special; he had none of the self-conscious crudity other boys of his age would have shown in the same situation.

"*Tu m' énerves,*' said Mic, and left me in peace at last.

When, on the following morning, I had a letter from my mother asking me how soon I planned to return to London, I had a strong urge to go immediately. I could easily say I had been called home. But by the time I had finished breakfast sitting at the battered table in the sun, the desire to leave Tréguinec had gone. It was a still hot day which started off faintly misty; the sea shimmered through it.

I would leave in a week's time; that would make my stay four weeks' long, roughly the time Mic had spent in London. Two months solid of each other's company; no wonder we were getting on each other's nerves.

Feeling tired and headachey, I drifted down later to Jean's café. He was busy clearing it up with his wife's help before they all went back to their home for the weekend. Laure sat on a stool eating ice-cream gloomily. Jean was tearing down paper decorations; one red streamer hung in untidy loops from the central light, looking like entrails.

'Move your fat self,' said Jean to Laure. 'If you're not going to help, go outside.' Laure picked up a cloth and languidly began to wipe tables. Jean looked bad-tempered and hot. I wandered off on to the beach, lay down on my towel and barely ticked over for the next hour. At one point I heard, miles away, vaguely familiar voices saying, 'She's asleep. Don't let's wake her,' and I couldn't summon enough energy even to twitch a finger. It was as if all my muscles were out of order; very enjoyable.

Some time later Joël settled himself beside me. I managed to lift one lid.

'Ai, ai, ai,' he yawned noisily. 'If you feel as I feel you feel awful.'

I tried to send little mice of energy to work my tongue, but nothing moved. After a long pause Joël said, 'You'll get sunstroke if you lie like that all morning.'

I sat up suddenly and my head was full of flashing fireworks.

'You're right. I feel ghastly.'

'Come for a swim. It'll freshen you up.'

The sea shocked my hot body, and I gasped and ran in and out to acclimitize myself. Then Joël and I swam out to a flat rock which was exposed at low tide, and lay down on our stomachs watching the beach. Every now and then we splashed water over ourselves.

'I've decided to go at the end of next week.'

'We're leaving then too.'

In the distance, fairground music started up. A coloured windmill advertising the fair and circus revolved in the sun. A few people drifted off the beach towards the fairground.

'I saw the Englishman go off with Antoine and Pierre this morning.'

'Thomas was due to leave today for Carnac.' The mention of Antoine gave me a sickening jolt.

'He's gone off with the other two in Antoine's car. They had luggage on the roof-rack.'

I sucked my salty knuckles and started to battle with that painful lump inside me. It had been there all morning after all. Joël went on talking, but I didn't hear him. About Antoine's departure I felt disappointment, even a little relief, but mostly emptiness and frustration. Everything was left so *untidy*. Perhaps he would be back again in a day's time, and I would see him. What I expected from this encounter I don't know; I just wanted to see him. I remembered the curious sensation of his lips on mine. Already in my memory this incident had gained romance, and though I mocked myself, I couldn't help or stop the romanticizing process.

A splashing near the rock surprised us, and there was Mic's grinning face.

'I hate to disturb you two,' she said, 'but that rock's public property. Shove up.' I stared balefully at Mic's face in the frothy green sea-water; she had a piece of weed wrapped round her neck, and when its end lifted in the water it looked like a snake. Joël leaned out to duck her, but she swam out of his reach with a powerful push of her legs. She climbed up on to the rock despite our lack of enthusiasm for her presence, and flopped down between us. We lay in silence in the sun, each busy with his own thoughts. Joël's looked as if they were mostly concerned with the speedy extermination of Mic. Suddenly he said, '*Ah, merde!*' and dived into the sea.

'Dear me. What's upset him?' said Mic.

'You have.'

She laughed. 'I find Joël ridiculous.'

He was swimming away from us fast and furiously, and his ungainly crawl style did look funny. We both giggled, though I felt a traitor.

'Your English friend has left with Antoine and Pierre. They've all gone to Carnac.'

'I know.'

'How the hell? They told me they didn't wake you to say goodbye.' So the vague voices I had heard were theirs. That was a small solace, at least.

'Joël told me. He saw them leave.'

'Oh, Joël.' She yawned. 'They called in to see my father's photographs of the destroyed dolmen. He gave Thomas one of them.'

I lay, cursing myself for having missed them. Mic continued to chatter, and when she realized I was not listening she pinched my arm.

'You're a sly one.'

'Look who's talking.'

'Go on, tell me what happened between you and Antoine last night. I know something did.'

'Use your fertile imagination, it'll be more interesting than the truth.'

'Very funny.' Mic's armour was thin this morning, and her distress showed for a moment. She clearly felt very left out of things. Mic was so tough it was easy to forget that she had feelings too.

'He was rude to me, that's all. Rude and sarcastic. You know how cutting he can be.'

She gazed at me assessing my explanation, suspicious of my friendly tone.

'He really did upset me, Mic.' The painful lump took over, and to my horror I felt tears pouring down my cheeks. I turned over on to my front, and burying my face in my arms I sobbed uncontrollably.

'*Zut alors,*' said Mic, overcome with embarrassment. 'O.K., O.K., I believe you.' She was not a girl who could cope with tears. 'I'll come back when you feel better.' She dived off the rock with a splash. I cried for a while longer, regretting the stupid futile mess of my first love. Then I rolled over on to my back and lay squeezing my eyelids shut to stop the flow of tears. They ran down the sides of my face into my ears, but they did stop. I sighed, shuddering a couple of times, and felt more in control. I lay trying not to think at all, because if I thought I thought only of Antoine, and my tears would start again. The painful lump, having expanded into the whole of me, subsided again until it was just an aching spot. I splashed my face with sea water and dived into the sea. Most people had left the beach for lunch; the Jouberts and Menards were gone; Françoise was still there, slowly drying herself and looking pensive. I avoided her eyes, but her mind was elsewhere and she paid little attention to me. My face felt swollen.

I heard a voice calling, 'Mary! Mary!' It was Angélique Menard. She stood at the top of the path, and called plaintively. '*A table!*'

'I'm coming.' My voice was unsteady.

I bounded up the cliff path, hoping Mic had been tactful for once and not told the assembled family about my fit of tears. As I slipped into my place at table I looked swiftly round; but no one took special notice of me, so I relaxed. I was unexpectedly overcome with a raging hunger, and ate everything offered me.

When we had reached the fruit and cheese Monsieur said, 'So you are leaving us at the end of the week?'

'Yes.'

'Your French is excellent.'

'My mother has always given me extra coaching—she studied French at university.'

'That explains it. Only a month in France would not give you such fluency.'

'Everyone's leaving,' said Mic gloomily. 'Françoise goes on Wednesday, the Lamartines on Thursday. The Jouberts are going at the weekend. Why do we have to stay another week?'

'My dear Marie-Claire, to keep you out of mischief in Paris.'

She glared at her father. He took no notice and turned to me. 'I saw your charming English friend this morning before he departed for Carnac. He's very knowledgeable. I gave him one of my photographs of the dolmen.'

'I'm sure he was pleased.'

'He was.' Monsieur was peeling an orange with neat finicky fingers. 'Inspired by my talk with him, I paid a visit this morning on the Baron Auguste de la Parmentière.' We all looked at him. 'We had an interesting talk. Very interesting.' His face impassive, he ate segments of his orange.

'Well, go on Philippe, what did he say?'

'He was polite. Yes, yes, he had destroyed the dolmen, after all there were quite enough dolmens in Brittany. Scholarship would not miss the demise of one. There was no other site possible for his helicopter, poor man, so he had no choice. Etcetera, etcetera, etcetera.' His voice grew angry, and we all waited for him to go on. He finished his orange first. 'I had great pleasure in telling him I would do my utmost to get him prosecuted. My utmost. Then I called him an unscrupulous desecrator and left.'

Gervaise drummed his fork on the table in approbation. '*Olé!* That'll give him something to think about.'

'Not at all,' said Monsieur drily. 'He obviously thought I was wasting my breath. Well, if he has friends in high places, so have I. I must see Antoine.'

'Antoine's left.'

'What do you mean?'

'He's gone to Carnac with the Englishman.'

'Blast.' Monsieur got up impatiently, and started to leave the dining-room.

'How would Antoine help you anyway?' said Madame.

'He knows the Baron slightly. Marie knows his ex-wife well. They might be able to tell me something useful about his background and his friends. I intend to get him.'

'You could contact Antoine in Paris.'

'True.' He hesitated, and then went off. The rest of the family started talking about Paris, about the start of school, about someone called Lisette who was keeping an eye on their apartment while they were *en vacance*. They lived behind the Boulevard Saint-Michel. The 'Boul' Miche' as Mic called it.

Somehow their life in Paris sounded in every way more interesting than mine in London. I thought of my winter ahead, of the dreadful freezing sessions on the games pitch, of crowded buses and tubes smelling of wet coats and shoes. Of getting up too early in the dark to put on my hated uniform, and the perpetual sniffle I seemed to have throughout the winter. I heard Mic say she was fed up with sharing a room, and Madame replied that after Christmas they would be renting two extra rooms on their floor so she would just have to wait till then. Christmas: the Menards always spent two weeks skiing at Christmas. They all began to discuss that, and I went up to my room as soon as I could. I wrote my parents a short boring letter telling them the details of my return. I felt discontented, and irritable; even my new clothes did nothing to cheer me up. I shut myself in my Breton bed and without quite meaning to, fell asleep.

My last week at Tréguinec was different in every way from the first three weeks. The weather became grey and stormy; the wind was strong, too strong to go sailing, too strong to sit in comfort on the beach. We would rush into the sea and swim in the choppy grey breakers, warm and frothing, and our brown faces looked even browner in the grey light. Then we would play volleyball, but the wind gave the ball a life of its own, and the game was three-sided until the wind won.

When you opened the door to Jean's café papers flapped and danced, and sand flew across the floor. The café was snug and warm, and we would drink hot coffee and play hilarious games of ping-pong. I felt mad and reckless; since Antoine was no longer there to offend or please, I was liberated. Whenever my painful lump showed signs of growing larger, I was even more gay and reckless.

Mic imported a friend from another group, a boy called Jean-Paul, whose friends had all gone back home. Joël and I, Mic and Jean-Paul, did everything together all day long; we played ping-pong, or cards, or stupid games like consequences, and laughed together about nothing. It was fun, cosy, and unreal; there was something unnatural about the sudden closeness of our foursome. The bad weather pushed us together, and we all knew the fun would end on Saturday, when both Jean-Paul and I were due to leave. I can't remember what Jean-Paul looked like, but he was *sympathique,* and his presence diluted Mic's acid.

On my last night we went to the cinema in the village; once a week a film was shown in the scruffy village hall, with long pauses between each reel. We saw an old American film with a name like *The Unsinkable Molly Brown* or some such; it was dubbed into French, which was badly done and made a bad film worse. The audience was noisy, and cheered or booed at appropriate moments; when the projector broke down everyone shouted advice. The projectionist leaned over his balcony and shouted something back which made the audience roar with laughter. Joël explained that he was the local postman, and had threatened to throw all their letters in the sea. There was a noisy exchange of

105

views on the subject while the fault in the projector was put right.

'What idiots,' said Mic. She jabbed Jean-Paul in the ribs. 'Get us some chocolate.' Jean-Paul, not having yet got Mic's measure, did so. By the time he came back the film had started again, and everyone hissed at him as he struggled through knees to his seat. Mic smiled sweetly at him, and ate most of the chocolate herself.

On the way back Joël made me lag behind the others. I was wary of an intense farewell scene; he was such a good friend I didn't want him to spoil it.

'Will you come back next year?'

'I expect so. If Mic comes to me.'

'If she doesn't, I'll come instead and then you can stay with us in exchange.'

'There's no room for an extra person in your villa, Joël.'

This was so true he was silent. After a pause he grabbed my hand. 'You must come back next year.'

'I want to come back very much.' Antoine's sardonic face was in my mind's eye. Joël held my hand tightly.

'I'm glad.'

I could not meet his eyes, and we walked on in silence, still holding hands. Mic and Jean-Paul went ahead, pushing each other into the bank. When Mic looked round for us I let Joël's hand go. By the time we got back to the Menards' it was eleven o'clock, and Monsieur and Madame were just going to bed. They had lit a fire in the big open grate in the dining-room, which was still smouldering. The room smelt of pungent woodsmoke. Monsieur gave us all a glass of sweet white wine, and said we could finish the bottle.

'But it's time they went to bed,' said Madame.

'It's Mary's last night,' pleaded Mic. 'One hour more. Just one hour.' Her parents sized her up.

'All right.' Madame sighed.

'The party is over at midnight, and not a minute

later. Understood?' Monsieur waggled his eyebrows in mock fierceness at us, put a straw hat on his head and minced out; he then peered at us through the dining-room windows, making ferocious expressions. Joël and I hooted with laughter, and Jean-Paul obviously thought Monsieur was a little touched in the brain.

'Philippe, you're a fool,' said Madame fondly, and led him off to bed.

Mic set up the record-player, and put on a record. But we didn't dance, because we suddenly felt shy, just the four of us in the dark dining-room late at night. Instead we played cards for a while, and then just sat and talked while we finished up the wine. The wind raged outside, almost gale-force. The sea was a mass of white breakers.

I knew which record I needed to hear before I left. We hadn't played it for over a week. Silence fell when *Ne me quitte pas* started, and we gave it our absolute attention, even Jean-Paul. I had come to love the song so much it almost hurt to listen to it. The singer celebrates and tries to forget, unsuccessfully, his love for a woman; and unless you also find a copy of the record and listen to it, you will never quite see why we found it so perfect and precious.

> *I will offer you pearls of rain*
> *Come from a country where rain does not exist,*
> *I will make a kingdom*
> *Where love is law*
> *And you will be queen.*
> *I will . . .*

It struck me that words like these will never be written by anyone for me; only a few lucky women know such celebration of love. Sitting there in that aromatic Breton room I was afraid that such fire would not come my way, however much I dreamed.

> *Moi je t' offrirai*
> *Les perles de pluie*

107

Venues de pays
Où il ne pleut pas . . .

I looked up and met Joël's green eyes watching me
intently.

7

The winter was better than I expected. My month in France had given me confidence, and things like a snub or a spot on my face did not bother me as they used to. I didn't tell a soul about my experiences in Brittany; they were too precious to hand around my gossiping school-friends, but their presence inside me was enough. I had a secret past now to my life, and secrets give you power. Boys at parties who never used to notice my existence did so now. The old cliché that nothing succeeds like success is only too true when it comes to popularity. I had longed to be popular; now that I was, it seemed unimportant.

I auditioned for the school play, which I had never done before for fear I would not get the part I wanted. We were doing *As You Like It,* and I willed the producer with all my might into choosing me to play Celia. They offered me Rosalind. I didn't know what to say and stood aghast; finally the producer said, 'Don't you want to play Rosalind?'

'Yes.'

'You're a dark horse, Mary Meredith.'

When I told my parents about my part, my mother was delighted. My father just said, 'I see.' Later in the evening he added, 'It would be too much to hope, I suppose, that this won't affect your A-levels.'

'I'll make sure it doesn't.' I got up every morning

and worked for an hour before breakfast. Since it was normally very difficult for me to get out of bed at all, my mother said I worried her.

The minor point that secretly bothered me about playing Rosalind was the realization I would have to wear tights and a doublet. I saw some exercises described in the Sunday paper designed to reduce particular parts of one's anatomy. I worked hard on those for 'waist, buttocks and thighs', but mine remained their usual prominent selves. I decided that my acting would have to be good enough to take the audience's attention off my girth.

To start with my acting was dreadful. During the first month of rehearsals I was so bad I thought my part would be taken away. The girl playing Celia was already good; bright and lively and sure of her lines. The boy playing Orlando also learned his lines quickly (I tried to invest him with romance by imagining he was Antoine). I was slow in learning my lines; I stumbled and muttered and forgot my moves. I overheard Mrs Drew, the producer, say to another teacher, 'I thought we'd made a discovery, but she's disappointing.' I knew she was talking about me by the way she smiled at me when she saw me nearby. I panicked.

That evening I asked my mother if she would go through the whole of my part with me, to help me learn my words. I felt embarrassed asking her, because knowing that she could hear how I performed Rosalind made me intensely shy. She looked pleased.

'We'll do it tonight.'

'It'll take hours.'

'Well, if we don't finish, we can do the rest tomorrow.'

I pushed a spoon in and out of the sugar. 'I *must* do it all tonight, or it may be too late. I'm afraid they'll give the part to someone else, I'm so bad.' Sugar shot all over the table. 'Hell, I'm sorry.' But my mother did not notice; her attention had been distracted by my little brother Frederick, making sick noises under

110

the kitchen table. I started to go up the stairs, and my mother having removed a raw potato from Frederick's mouth, called after me, 'We'll start after supper, darling, and go on all night if necessary.' Then she winked at me. 'Luckily Robin's at a dinner tonight, so he won't be back until late. We'll have the place to ourselves.'

When she winked like that, she looked quite young. I went upstairs, trying to remember how old she was. Thirty-six, or thirty-seven, I couldn't remember which. It wasn't very old, after all, only five years older than Antoine. To think I had fallen in love with someone nearly of my mother's age gave me a shock.

I sat down in front of the gas fire in my bedroom and thought about Antoine. 'Thinking about Antoine' was a special activity which I got down to rather with the same deliberation I would eat a meal or read a book. I realized that I could hardly remember his face; but the tone of his voice was clear in my mind's ear. I thought of the silver chain on his brown wrist, of his extraordinary blue eyes. I wondered what he was doing, as I had wondered a hundred times. He would be in the middle of his university term, busy lecturing to his students; a far cry from the idle summer in Brittany. He wouldn't have thought about me since then once, while I'd thought about him for hours and hours. I reached to open the drawer in my bedside table to get out the photographs I had taken of the crowd on the beach. I did it one day when Antoine was there, and managed to include him, as if incidentally, in most of the snaps. They were not very clear, because something is wrong with the focus of my camera and, maddeningly, in the clearest Mic's hand making a rude gesture is obscuring half Antoine's face. He is actually smiling towards the camera, so Mic's forever recorded gesture is particularly annoying. I stared at his pictured face and was disappointed that I felt nothing.

A tap on my door made me jump and shove the photograph away. My mother came straight in so she

111

must have seen this, but she gave no sign. She was carrying a bottle of cider and two glasses.

'This will keep us going.' She hovered. 'Where do you want me to sit?'

'Oh, Mum, anywhere.' I couldn't have wanted less to go through my part, and my mother's kind interest annoyed me. Feeling mean, I tried to banish my irritation. 'You sit on the bed.' She curled up and padded the wall with pillows.

'Give me your script.'

'No, you take this.' I handed her the complete Shakespeare.

'No, Mary, give me yours, and you do it without the words.'

'Cripes.'

'You must. You'll never learn it otherwise.' We started off. Mum was so matter-of-fact and funny, reading all my cues, that I stopped feeling a fool almost at once. By the time she'd finished taking me through all my speeches until I was word perfect, it was almost midnight. We were sitting satisfied but exhausted, sipping cider, when my father came in.

'A dormitory feast, I see. Where are the sardines?' He sat down on my bed with us and rubbed his hands roughly over his face. 'Aah, I'm tired.'

'We're tired too. I've been going through Mary's part with her all evening.'

'Do you realize how late it is?'

'Yes. We were just going to bed.' We all yawned, one after another, and then sat slumped and unmoving for some minutes. The gas fire popped softly. After a minute or two my father began to snore. Mum giggled, and tweaked his ear. He opened his eyes, staggered to his feet, and dragged her off the bed after him.

'Go to bed, Mary. You'll be good for nothing in the morning,' he said. As they reached the door, Mum turned and added, 'Don't get up early, for once.'

'All right.'

They went down the stairs murmuring and laughing

together; they talked in their bedroom for ages, because I heard the noise though not the words. It occurred to me that their life together was unknown to me, and always would be. Perhaps all the people you know are absolute strangers except when they are in the room with you. With these profound thoughts I went to bed, full of a real relief that I knew my part at last.

It was from this point onwards I became sure that if I did eventually want to go on the stage, I had got what it takes. My acting of Rosalind became better and better; she was both myself, and a friend I spent all my time with and knew more deeply than I could ever know a human friend. But what interested me was the effect I had on other members of the cast. Those who had real acting ability developed as I did, and we found it rewarding to act with each other; but those like the girl playing Celia, whose gift was really mimicry, showed up more and more as empty prattlers. They were effective superficially, but their performances did not develop. I hated my conversations with Celia, and as they took up a large part of the play, I knew that the production would be a failure. Celia was so frothy, and did something different every time, so there was never anything to build on. At the end of one rehearsal the girl playing Celia, Moira Fitchett, said angrily to me,

'Why do you always look at me as if I smell or something?'

'I'm frightfully sorry—I never meant . . .'

'You think you're so marvellous. I think your acting is just plain stodgy.' Out she flounced. Her father was a writer of some kind, a fact she often reminded us of. He often collected Moira from rehearsal; he wore a black fur hat like a Cossack's and called Moira by a nickname which sounded like Poodle and which she clearly did not want us to hear. She was always fashionably dressed, and was taken on summer holidays to places like Morocco. I used to be very envious of her.

When we came to perform the play, we did it badly. Moira had made up her mind to be the best thing in it, and invented so many new moves and inflexions that she threw the rest of us off our stride. I was utterly fed up with her, but there was nothing anyone could do; she thought she was marvellous. I knew her gyrations detracted from my performance, but I did not change it, and acted the best I could. The whole affair was utterly depressing, a frustrating waste of effort. Mrs Drew told Moira she had ruined the play by her selfish performance.

'Some people thought I was the best thing in it.'

'They were wrong.' Mrs Drew looked upset, and said no more to Moira. But when she told us all that she was putting me forward for the National Youth Theatre, there was a dreadful scene. Moira could not believe she was not being put forward as well, and hated me so much she was hardly sane. She destroyed an essay of mine, and defaced some of my books. I began to be afraid of her. Luckily, her parents removed her at Christmas, and sent her to a well-known drama school.

At about the time the play was performed, I had letters from Mic and Joël, both containing newspaper cuttings. These described the arrest of Baron Auguste de la Parmentière for smuggling drugs into England and America, using his home on the coast of Brittany as a base for operations. Even at this distance from Paris, I felt excited and curious about the exact details of how he was caught. Mic said her father had reported the destruction of the dolmen, and this may have aroused the interest of the authorities. Monsieur Menard was annoyed, she added, because now there was little point in a second prosecution over the dolmen when the drug trial would obviously be a *cause célèbre*.

I was surprised that our casual suspicions about the Baron had been so accurate. I promptly sat down and wrote first to Mic, and then a longer letter to Joël, discussing the whole business. I owed Joël a letter anyway; his last letter to me, stiff and rather shy in tone, had ended with a PS saying, 'I think of you often. Do you think of me?' I did not know what to reply. Joël: when I considered it, I suppose I did think of him, but in an involuntary way. Things he had said, or expressions of his, would flash through my mind, or sometimes linger unexpectedly. But I didn't make a mental meal of him as I did of Antoine. I deliberately tried to relive all the good moments I had spent with or near Antoine; it was a ritual. Yet without meaning to, I would often remember Joël's arrival on the moonlit beach when I was swimming, and his kindness afterwards, and his sympathetic eyes, blacky green in the dark; and his arms around me, comforting me and himself. It was hard to write to Joël. I wrote several letters to Antoine, but of course tore them up.

So I was pleased to have something special to write to Joël about, and I hoped he would not notice that I avoided answering his question. My letter was long and friendly, and I got an equally long one back by return. From then on we wrote frequently to each other. I began to long for Joël's letters; the initial shyness now gone, he wrote long, funny letters, lively and interesting, and drew quaint humpy drawings of people and places. Like Euclid my frog, they had a dotty charm, and I loved them. (I had Euclid II on my shelf.) If you write regularly to someone, your correspondence becomes a conversation; and as each letter opens more ideas, so you have more to say. When anything happened, it wasn't complete until I had described it to Joël.

It became an effort to think about Antoine; by Christmas I hardly thought of him at all.

I was given a generous record-token for Christmas from my grandmother, and went down to one of the big stores in Oxford Street on a cold January day to try and buy Jacques Brel singing *Ne me quitte pas*. I felt a hunger to hear it, to have my summer reinvoked.

I explained the record to a salesgirl, but she had no idea what I was talking about and called over a confident young man. He ignored me, and said in a tired voice to the girl, 'If it's not in the foreign vocal section we haven't got it.'

'She says she can't find it.' They both looked in my direction.

'I can't find Jacques Brel at all.'

'Who?'

'Jacques Brel. He's a French singer.' The young man stared at me disapprovingly, and I felt my face going red. 'If you haven't got it I'd like to order it.'

'If it's a record manufactured in France it will take a long time to come.'

I suddenly lost my temper. 'Don't you want to sell any records?'

'You are a very rude young girl.'

'And you're very unhelpful.'

'Take this child's order,' he said to the salesgirl, who had stood tapping with her long nails on the glass counter throughout our conversation, her eyes blank.

'Don't bother.' I walked away, my dignity lowered by the fact I knew I looked like a schoolgirl. I was so angry I wanted to cry. A touch on my arm made me jump; a strange man smiled hesitantly at me. He looked vaguely familiar.

'You'll find all the Jacques Brel records you want in a shop I know in Tottenham Court Road. They specialize in French music.' He wrote the name down on the back of an envelope he took from his pocket.

'There you are. Try them.' He smiled again, and went off into the depths of the shop.

My spirits renewed, I hurried down the length of Oxford Street. The wind was icy, and seemed to use the street as a funnel. Turning into Tottenham Court Road was a relief, and I found the shop at once. They had several Brel records, including the long prayer with *Ne me quitte pas* on it. I was so pleased I couldn't stop smiling, and while they wrapped my record up, I turned over the envelope the man had given me. I saw written on it:

116

John Sands Esq
c/o The Observer
160 Queen Victoria Street, EC4.

Sands: that was why he seemed familiar, he had looked very like Thomas Sands. Perhaps he was a brother or cousin. I also remembered the name John Sands as one of the music critics whom my father admired because he always talked such good sense. Excited by the coincidence, I hurried to the tube. Thomas Sands lived in London; he had given me his telephone number and told me to ring him any time I felt like it, particularly if I had special news about Tréguinec and the dolmen. I had forgotten all about him, but I was sure he would be interested in the Baron's arrest, so I rang him up that evening. For a moment he obviously had not a clue who I was.

'We met last summer in Tréguinec.'

'Of course. Of course. How nice to hear your voice.' A female voice said something in the background, and he laughingly said, 'Don't be ridiculous,' to someone who giggled. His voice came back to me, and he said in jolly tones, 'Well, well, what's your news?'

I told him all about the Baron, and he sounded surprised and interested. After I'd finished he said slowly,

'So it's unlikely anyone will bother to prosecute on the destruction of the dolmen as well.'

'Mic said her father did not think it was worth it.'

'I hope Menard pursues it nevertheless.' There was a pause while he dealt with a query from the female voice in the background. 'I'm using one of Menard's photographs in my book, by the way. It's reproduced very well.'

'When will your book be published?'

'Some time next summer.' I wondered if he had remembered his promise to mention me in the foreword, but was almost sure he had forgotten.

'How's life treating you, Mary?'

'O.K.'

117

'At school, I suppose. Working very hard?'

'Yes.'

He sounded different, brisk and busy. There was a pause, before he said, 'Well, you must come and see us some time.'

'I'd love to.' I wondered who 'us' was, and as if he sensed my question he explained,

'I got married this autumn. Swept off my feet and up to the altar in less than a month.' I heard a soft laugh in the background.

'Oh. Congratulations.' I didn't know what to say: people I knew didn't get married, because they were either married already or my own age. After a short pause I said, 'By the way, is the music critic John Sands anything to do with you?'

'My brother. Why?'

'Oh, he gave me some directions . . .' I started a rather garbled account of my encounter with John Sands but Thomas interrupted.

'So John has been picking up schoolgirls. I must take him to task.'

'No, no . . .'

'Well, Mary, promise you'll give us a ring and come and have tea with us one Sunday?'

But I knew as I promised that I wouldn't, and that he didn't specially want me to. I went up to my room rather depressed by the whole conversation with Thomas. On my bed I saw my new record, lying so far unplayed. I was waiting until supper was over, and my own private evening upstairs began. No one would interrupt me now, so I put the record on, turned the lights off, and lay down by the bright gas fire. The record hissed quietly, and the room was full of vivid music and that harsh beautiful voice; it was all so dramatic and emotional compared with English popular music. For a few minutes the effect was so overwhelming I felt almost uncomfortable. Then my ears got used to the style again, and I waited as song after song drew me nearer to the one I longed to hear. After not hearing it for four

118

months, *Ne me quitte pas* was even better than I remembered it, poignant and aching. My eyes filled with tears and I went cold all over at its beauty. When the air was silent, I reached for my pen and wrote to Joël.

8

One day just before Easter as I wandered slowly out of our gate, I noticed how black and grimy the laurel bushes were, squashed into the small front garden. A thick layer of black smuts had collected on the leaves over the winter; I rubbed one between my fingers and it felt gritty. My fingers came away blackened. Poor laurels, I wondered how they breathed at all; I would hose them down and clean them. Not today, but some time soon. I shut the gate, and stood indecisive about which way to walk. The day was soft and clear, the sort of spring day that's so beautiful you can't think of anything to do that's good enough for it. For want of a better idea, I decided to wander across the Common. I looked back at the bushes: the pale clear sun made them look like dirty tramps, particularly against the delicate new leaves and yellow flowers of the forsythia.

'Mary.' I was in a dream, because I distinctly heard Joël's voice. Again it came, hesitantly this time, like a question, 'Mary?' I swung round, and there he was.

I can't find the right words to describe this extraordinary moment. Nothing had prepared me for the sight of Joël; it was as if I had looked down and found, against all possibility, I had three legs instead of two.

'Vraiment, c'est moi.' He came and stood near me; his French made him real. I took his outstretched hand.

'Joël. I can't believe it.' I spoke in English. We both stood there, grinning at each other like fools; the rest of the world stopped existing. *'Ce n'est pas possible.'* My French sounded rough on the tongue.

He was much taller than I remembered, his dark red hair was more vivid, his green eyes more striking. It was as if I had only kept a pale shadow of the real Joël in my memory; now that he stood before me, his whole being hit me like a force.

'Your hair's so golden,' he said. I think he was experiencing the same feelings of shock. I laughed, and he laughed too.

'But how have you suddenly appeared, like magic?'

'My family are in Calais for Easter visiting my grandmother. It was too good an opportunity to miss, so I took the boat, hitchhiked, and here I am.' He was wearing jeans, a jersey, and an anorak, and his only luggage was a duffle bag.

'Come in.' I swung the gate open. He looked up at our house—we live in a Georgian house in Clapham, which my father inherited.

'So this is Pepys Lodge I've been writing to all the winter.' He looked impressed, and I was glad the paintwork was peeling and the front door scuffed. It's a beautiful historic house, but is inclined to give people a false idea of our income. The entrance hall is full of push chairs, tricycles, large tin cars; the sort of paraphernalia my two brothers collect around them.

'There's no one at home at the moment. My mother has taken Stephen and Frederick to the Zoo.'

'You were just going out?'

'Only for a walk by myself.'

'I'll come too.'

We dumped his bag in a push chair, and set off across the Common. I couldn't help feeling the day had grown even finer, though I now paid little attention to it. The fact we were talking in French put a barrier between me and London. Joël and I resumed conversation where we'd left off in our last letters.

'How were your tests?'

'O.K. I didn't do too badly. And you?'

He shrugged. 'I'm fed up with the Bac. Our whole lives are run by it. Exams shouldn't be so important. Enough of school, let's not talk about it. What's this park we're in?'

'Clapham Common.'

'It's very big.'

'London has much bigger parks and commons. I'll take you to Hyde Park and Green Park—they're right in the centre.' I felt excited by the prospect of taking Joël round London. 'I'll show you everything.'

'I can only stay four days.'

'Oh. Never mind, I might not have had you here at all.'

Joël ran ahead to pick up a stray ball, which he threw back with a graceful arc of his body. It wasn't only that he had grown taller; he had filled out, and his body was no longer a boy's. The aura of his physical presence was not as I remembered either; the difference was hard to pin down, and pleasantly disturbing.

'Shall we go sight-seeing now? We've got all afternoon. Are you tired?'

'I'm never tired. Let's go.'

We took an 88 bus through the heart of London. We got off in Oxford Street, walked back down Regent Street, across Piccadilly, down via the Mall into Green Park. We walked right through to Westminster Abbey, when I suddenly became aware of the time. We had talked so much that time had stopped existing. Feeling very tired suddenly, I worked out the best way to get home. I hoped supper was stretchable; seven o'clock on Good Friday was not an ideal time to introduce a guest to my parents.

We sat in silence in the bus. Our bodies and our tongues were tired. All Joël said was, 'Will your mother mind me staying?'

'She'll be pleased.'

'And your father?' He looked nervous.

'I never know what he's going to think.'

We said no more until we reached our gate, when Joël looked at his watch. 'We should have come back earlier.'

'Yes, I know, but don't worry. My parents won't eat you.'

When I opened the front door, there was the usual bed-time racket going on; Stephen grizzling in the kitchen (Stephen's five) and Frederick wailing away upstairs, penned in his cot. Joël's duffle bag had been put on the hall table in an obvious position, as if it was a question mark in itself.

'Stephen, go back to bed this instant, and someone will come and mend your light.' My mother sounded cross, to say the least. 'I think I heard the front door— go and see if Mary's back, will you, Stephen. On your way upstairs.'

Stephen appeared at the end of the hall looking foul-tempered. His expression became blankly wary when he saw us. His pyjama bottoms hung at half mast, and he was holding the old piece of blanket he still insisted on sleeping with.

'Mum.' I went into the kitchen before Stephen could say anything. 'A French friend of mine has arrived out of the blue. Can we put him up for a few days?' She didn't turn round from the chopping board at first, so I went on, to put her in the picture, 'He's here in the hall now. He's come specially to see me. He's a friend of the Menards.' I heard my father's footsteps coming down the stairs; I heard him saying good evening to Joël before he appeared in the kitchen, bringing Joël with him.

'I found this fellow in the hall looking lost, tired and hungry. What a host you are, Mary.'

'He's French,' I began.

'I gathered that.'

'He's just arrived in London . . .'

'All the more reason for food and drink. What would you like to drink?' He turned to Joël, who was

124

totally confused by now. I explained, and in the end he went off to have a bath first of all. I showed him where everything was and as I was about to leave him he said, 'Your mother wasn't very pleased to see me.'

'Yes, she was. She's tired, that's all—by the end of a day of looking after those two little monsters, anyone would be tired.'

Joël smiled. He swung the light switch to and fro. The bath was full of plastic toys, but I thought he could cope with that. Stephen's head appeared round a door.

'Go to bed. That's my brother Stephen. The other one, Frederick, is only two.'

When I spoke French Stephen stared at me in amazement. 'Why are you gabbling like that, Mary?'

'I'm talking French to Joël because he is French. Go to bed. I'll come and tuck you in.'

I went downstairs to help, and heard my mother talking in a low voice to my father; she stopped when I went in and gave me a vague smile.

'I hope your friend isn't used to French grand cuisine because it's very much a scratch supper.'

'He won't mind a bit. What can I do to help?'

'Lay the table if you like.'

My father said casually, 'What time did Joël arrive?'

'This afternoon, earlyish.' He appeared to need amplification so I went on, 'We went and did some sightseeing. He's never been to London before and he's only got four days here.'

'You didn't expect him?'

'Not at all.' I explained how Joël had come to make his sudden trip. We talked in those light tones which our family is apt to use when we want to appear noncommittal but in fact learn something.

'Well, we're delighted to meet him,' said my mother, drinking her vermouth. Her temper was much improved. 'Does he speak any English?'

'Quite a bit, I think, only he's never been to England before so his ear isn't very used to the sound of it.'

We spoke a mixture of English and French at supper. My mother's French is still first-rate and she and Joël got on very well. He said later, as we talked upstairs, that he found her very *sympathique,* in the French sense.

'She's also very intelligent.'

I looked surprised. 'I suppose she is.'

'By the way, does your family ever get news of Antoine?'

'Antoine?' Joël was puzzled.

'Antoine Malmaison.'

'Oh, no. He's not a special friend of theirs.'

'I thought he was. They seemed very friendly last summer.'

'They are at Tréguinec. But in Paris Antoine moves in quite different circles.'

'What, university ones?'

Joël hesitated. 'His wife is very chic, very rich.'

'She won't be too happy to hear of her friend the Baron's activities.'

'I expect she knew all the time.'

'Go on.'

'These rich people.' Joël sat in silence, looking gloomy. Then he said, 'Actually, I don't suppose she did know, because rumours we heard said the Baron was in big-time smuggling.'

'I must say it's very gratifying to think we suspected him.'

Joël shrugged, indifferent. 'To be honest, I didn't really believe our suspicions. I wanted something to do. It seemed an amusing theory at the time, it gave us an excuse for exploring his property.' He sat forward. 'Mary, don't you find, when you think of last summer, that we were still children then, and we aren't any more? The me of last summer seems a completely different person.'

'By the end of last summer I had already changed.'

'I find you different now.'

'That's because . . .'

'Mary.' My mother called me from the stairs. I went to see what she wanted. 'You must let that boy go to bed, it's late and he looks exhausted. So do you.'

'All right.' When I got to my room I didn't feel sleepy at all, though my legs were tired after all the walking. I felt on edge and at war with myself. I put a jazz record on, but that made me feel worse. Maybe it was the talk of Antoine that had depressed me; I switched my mind to Antoine but my attention slipped off him as if he had been a slippery rock. My thoughts were arid. I sat down on my bed and took my clothes off; I was grimy after hours spent in London streets, but I had no energy left to bath. I washed my hands and face and went to bed as I was. When I lay down my bones tingled unpleasantly and I had to shift my position again and again. I was afraid I was in for a sleepless night; it was only in the last year I had begun to experience insomnia and I disliked it. But at least since the onset of occasional sleepless nights I had stopped having a recurrent nightmare which I have dreamt once or twice a year ever since I can remember. Sleepless nights were a small price to pay for the loss of that terror. It was a stifling nightmare, full of heat, and a certain pulsing crushing smell-noise; as the climax came I would be crushed by huge wedges of blackness and colour which sometimes resembled the legs of vast animals, thick like an elephant's. I would wake at this point sweating and literally terrified. But the worst thing about the nightmare was that indescribable crushing smell-noise; once I sensed it in half-sleep, I knew that nothing would stop the nightmare from running its course.

While thinking about my nightmare, I must have fallen asleep. Perhaps because my conscious mind had suggested it to my dreaming self, that night I had the nightmare again. But it was not quite the same, and though I woke up in a sweat as shapes crushed me, this time I felt I had beaten the nightmare. That smell-noise had almost vanished. My fear during the nightmare had been a fake, as if I had humoured it by getting frightened as usual. A great relief seeped through me. I thought of Bunyan's Burden, which I had always imagined as a horrid itchy growth of flesh; when it slipped off Christian's back it must have left a cool patch and a sense of delicious relief. This is exactly how I felt now.

When I woke up next morning every bit of me was happy. The house smelt of coffee and croissants warming; my mother sometimes made them for breakfast at weekends and their sweet buttery smell was the best start to a day. I lay still, content, my nose just poking up out of the warm water of semi-sleep. I heard hesitant footsteps going past the door. Of course, Joël was here. In a flash I was out of bed; I flung on some clothes and went downstairs within minutes. Joël was sitting at the large kitchen table, being examined by Stephen and Frederick. He was sitting in my father's chair, which made it more difficult to believe he was real. I had to put my hand on his shoulder as I went past him.

My father came in from the garden where he had been staring in fixed abstraction at a flowerbed.

'I'm determined to paint the bathroom today. I actually feel like it, so I'm off to buy some paint.'

The bathroom was in a particularly tatty state, because Stephen and Frederick had bashed the walls with a hammer. My father had put plaster in the holes, and they stood out against the original blue paintwork.

Mum suggested that Joël and I went off for the day somewhere, but when Joël saw my father carrying tins of paint and brushes upstairs, he insisted on helping and refused to go out at all. He said he liked painting. He put on an old pair of my father's pyjamas over his clothes, and stuck a battered old bowler hat on his head. Dad was similarly dressed, though his hat was a flat tweed cap, very aged and moth-eaten.

I felt cross at being deprived of Joël for the day, and at being excluded. When my mother suggested I tidied my room, I knew the croissants for breakfast had not, for once, augured a good day. As I passed the open door of the bathroom I saw Joël standing astraddle the bath painting the ceiling. His freckled face and green eyes stood out with special clarity against the pure white. He grinned and winked at me.

'You're getting on fantastically quickly.'

'Masses to do yet,' said my father, painting the window jamb with a careful but slightly shaking brush. A white bulge appeared on the glass. 'Damn.'

I went on downstairs, and found my mother reading the newspaper in the kitchen. The boys were playing in the sandpit at the end of the garden, and all was temporarily peaceful. Mum cast a vague eye at me over the paper, and said, 'How are the workers doing?'

'Getting on fast.' I sat down at the kitchen table and cut up a piece of orange peel with a knife while busy with my thoughts. I thought Mum had returned to her reading, and jumped when she said, 'I adore that boy, your Joël. He is utterly nice.'

I stared at her, not knowing what to say. I could feel myself blushing with pleasure.

'He must come and stay again, for longer.'

'I'll ask him.'

'Explain again who he is and how you came across him. I've forgotten what you originally said.'

So I explained the holiday set-up at Tréguinec, and described the various families.

'What enormous families they all have.'

'Four or five children is common.'

'Joël's one of five, then?'

'Yes—no, I think it's six. Suzanne, Marcel, Emmanuelle, Dominique, Pish and Joël. Yes, six. Pish is the baby, I don't know what her real name is.'

'Patrice perhaps.'

129

'That's a boy's name.'

'Oh. I always took it that the Menard child called Patrice was a girl.'

'He and Etienne are real little blighters.'

'Like ours? Or worse.'

'In another class of evil altogether.' Mum laughed. 'Mic is a devil, and they have the same streak.'

'Yes, I could see Mic is a devil. I'm not sure I would trust her.'

'Not an inch. She's the most unreliable person I know. But she's interesting. I like her even though she drove me mad by the end.' I had never discussed my friends with my mother before, and it was fun.

'Does Joël like her?'

I shrugged. 'Yes and no. They've known each other all their lives. She drives him mad too but no more than she does the rest of us. She teases him a lot.' I thought about Mic; I could recall her face vividly. 'Jean, the nice man who runs the café I told you about, said one day he was sure Mic's character would bring her a lot of unhappiness.'

My mother gazed at me half surprised, half speculatively. She said nothing, and after a few minutes of abstraction, returned to her newspaper.

Some hours later I went up to the bathroom and found Joël on his own, slowly wiping paint off a tap.

'You must stop, Joël.'

'What's the time?'

'Nearly six.'

'*Mon dieu.* No wonder I feel tired.' He stretched and looked with pride round the bathroom. 'I've enjoyed doing this. Being a painter would be a good job to have in many respects.'

'You'd get bored with it.'

'Not if you always did it well. And it affords lots of time for thought.' He sounded as if he was interested in it for himself.

'Don't be mad, Joël. I thought you wanted to be an ecologist or something.'

130

'Yes, of course I do. But it's foolish to think that would necessarily be a better job for me than painting houses.' He started to rub his hands with turps substitute, using a filthy painting cloth.

'It would be a waste if you painted houses.'

'Waste of what?'

'Your education, for a start.'

'I can still use it.' He took off the bowler hat, and shook his remarkable red hair. 'I think it would be a waste if you became an actress.'

'But I've discovered I'm good . . .'

'I don't doubt it.'

I stared at him, angry and puzzled that he should suddenly question my dream. I heard my voice become querulous as I said, 'Well, then, why don't you want me to become an actress? Tell me why.'

'I didn't say I didn't *want* you to, I just said it would be a waste.'

'One could take the view it would be a waste if I didn't.'

'I can't help it, I can't help feeling that the interpretative arts are second-rate.'

'*Second-rate*. What about great musicians?'

'Don't get so angry. I don't mean second-rate in *value,* but second-rate in *kind.*'

'What's the difference?' I was angry.

'There's a lot of difference. Interpretative artists may be superb, but they depend on another's creation. They'd be nothing without it. That's why they're second-rate.'

'I think you're wrong.' But I couldn't marshal any arguments, and Joël laughed at me. By this time we had moved out of the bathroom on to the landing outside. 'Anyway, why shouldn't I be first-rate at a second-rate occupation?'

'You've got something more to offer.'

'What, for instance?'

He looked helpless. 'I don't know. It's just a hunch.

131

Besides, I think you've got the wrong sort of temperament.'

This new tack left me staring at him in silence. The conversation came to an abrupt end because my father appeared, cleaned of paint and looking very spruce.

'We're all going out to dinner,' he said. 'Georgina and I have decided it would be a fitting reward for Joël's magnificent efforts.'

Joël did not follow him, so he repeated himself slowly. Having dinner in a restaurant with my parents is a rare treat, and the pleasure of the prospect made me forget our argument, at least for the moment. I went off to change, and as I was brushing my hair I wondered again what Joël meant by my temperament being wrong for an actress. I had enjoyed acting in the school play, hadn't felt in the least I was going against the grain. While we were waiting for my mother to finish briefing the babysitter, I asked Joël again what he meant.

He hesitated. 'You're not naturally narcissistic.' I gazed at him in surprise. 'Nor are you ruthless enough. Look, I've told you about my cousin Elisabeth. She's doing well on the stage, but believe me she's a tough cookie.'

'I'll get tougher.'

'She was ruthless when she was a child. You haven't got it in you.'

I went on staring at him, puzzled and disappointed.

'Mary, don't look so upset—it's a *good* thing you're not tough and vain like Elisabeth. I wouldn't love you if you were.'

The words he had just said lay in the air between us, as we stared silently at each other. Then my mother came in with the babysitter, a nice girl who lived round the corner.

'Well, Wendy, you know how the television works. Make yourself tea, coffee, anything you like.'

'Yes, all right, thanks.'

132

Under cover of the chatter, as we collected ourselves in the hall, I said quickly to Joël, still in French,

'Are you afraid I'll change if I go on the stage?'

'Of course. It's a corrupting world.'

'Away at last,' said my mother, as we joined my father, outside fuming in the car. The babysitter smiled at us through the window before drawing the curtains.

'I wonder if she pinches some booze,' said my father. 'Wouldn't put it past her. The innocent nice girls are always the ones to purloin the tipple.' My mother laughed.

'Well, the boys like her, so she's worth an extra half glass of whisky.'

We settled ourselves in the car and drove towards Chelsea, where my father had booked a table at his favourite restaurant. He had only taken me there once before.

Joël took my hand as we drove over Chelsea Bridge.

'You've got paint in your ear,' I said. He grinned, unmoved.

'There,' said my mother, 'that's the Royal Hospital, built by Christopher Wren. The most beautiful building in London.'

'In your opinion,' said my father. We drove slowly past its elegant symmetry, lying at an oblique angle to the road. 'But it is a superb building.' The bricks looked almost black in the dusk against the white paintwork.

On Easter Sunday my parents drove us to Burghclere to see the Stanley Spencer murals before we all had lunch with friends of theirs who lived on the river near Pangbourne. The weather stayed perfect, and as we reached the countryside beyond Maidenhead Joël saw it in ideal conditions. He was the sort of person you could show round for ever; eager, never fulsome, interested in different ways in everything, even in things he didn't like. He wasn't sure he liked the Stanley

133

Spencers, but he gave them all his attention. For once Stephen and Freddie, who usually ruined any outing, behaved quite passably.

We had lunch with the Forsyths. I hadn't been to the house for ages, but the family had come to London to stay with us a couple of years before. The only thing I remembered clearly about the house was the huge green paper fish which hung from the ceiling in the twins' playroom. The twins, girls, were now twelve but taller than I was. When I asked them about the fish they looked blank. Then one remembered.

'Oh, yes. The fish. We burned it at Guy Fawkes years ago.' They both went off straight after lunch to a pony club meet.

It was so fine we helped the Forsyths put their croquet hoops up, and Joël and I spent the whole afternoon playing croquet against my father and Mr Forsyth. Sometimes a game is exactly the right thing to do, and that afternoon croquet was what suited our mood. We laughed and bashed opponents' balls into bushes, and for once no one got bored and spoiled the game. When it was over Joël and I walked up and down the river bank.

'But England is so beautiful,' said Joël. We spoke French again.

'Didn't you expect it to be?'

'The French have a very incorrect picture of England and the English.'

'I shouldn't judge the English by what you've seen today.'

Joël shook his head. 'But no, any family is as representative as any other.'

'The Forsyths are rich. Most people aren't.'

'I wasn't thinking of material surroundings. For instance, those two girls are more typical of what the Frenchman thinks an English girl is like. Tall, cold, and addicted to horses.'

I laughed. 'They're a bit extreme those two. In fact,

134

they never stop reading books about horses and ponies. They're not typical of the girls I know.'

'I'd hate you to be horsey.'

I laughed at the idea. We sat for a while on a tree trunk, deliberately left at the river's edge as a seat. Ducks scooted near us; a bearded man in a rowing boat went past, seeming to travel at great speed because he moved with the flow of the water.

'One day,' said Joël dreamily, 'our problem will be to decide where to live, France or England.'

'Six months in each,' I said, as lightly as he had. Our eyes met, and he was about to say something more, when the Forsyths' dog ran up to us, and my mother and Mrs Forsyth appeared. Joël patted the dog, who ignored him.

'There is where we intend to build the boat-house,' said Mrs Forsyth, standing near us. My mother touched a mature willow, a large tree partly overhanging the water.

'What about this fine tree?'

'Well, we'll have to cut it down, which is sad.' We all stared at the willow, whose leaves were just beginning to show.

'Surely you could put the boat-house somewhere else, further up?' said my mother.

'For a selection of reasons, that's the only place suitable.' Mrs Forsyth spoke dampingly, but my mother, who loved trees, did not give in.

'You mustn't cut this tree down. It's taken thirty years to grow. It's an exquisite shape.'

'Fergus! Come here.' Mrs Forsyth called her awful dog. 'Well, Georgina, I know it's unfortunate, but the decision's made now and the plans drawn up.' She walked on along the bank. My mother looked strained; watching her, it occurred to me that she was not at her ease with Mrs Forsyth. She stroked the tree, frowning; Mrs Forsyth dithered back, smiling brightly.

'You always were such a romantic, Georgina,' she

began. Stephen appeared at that moment and said furiously,

'Mummy, you never got my ball out of the car. Come and get it.'

'In a minute.'

'Come *now*.'

'Be quiet, Stephen. I'm talking to Mrs Forsyth.'

Stephen started to cry and stamp his feet. Mrs Forsyth obviously itched to murder him; my mother looked exhausted.

'I'll get the ball for him,' I said nobly. 'Come on, Stephen.'

'No. I want Mummy . . .' I dragged him off by the ear. He is a poisonous little boy, but so are all children. It was a relief to feel I had moved clear of that category. Joël followed me. Being possessed of horrid small brothers himself he hardly noticed Stephen's and Freddie's existence. Though no one could call Dominique horrid; it occurred to me as I led Stephen forcibly to the car that both Joël and he had the same sweetness of nature. To describe this quality only makes it seem dull; bad qualities are easy to describe, and are immediately vivid for you on the page, but good qualities like Joël's kind humorous *caring* for people come across without their true strength.

'Not *that ball*. The red one.'

'Stephen, if you don't stop screaming at me, I shall shut you in the car.'

He didn't so I did. Joël and I sat on the steps of an old mounting block.

'Why do children get in such a state? It's so exhausting,' I said gloomily. A few minutes later I saw Stephen's rage had subsided; he was sitting in the driver's seat, playing with all the switches on the dashboard and turning the steering wheel. He didn't want to come out.

Joël and I leaned back against the sun-warmed wall. Above us the silence was broken by an engine; a small helicopter passed overhead.

136

'Tréguinec seems a million miles away,' I said dreamily.

'You will come next summer?'

'Of course. I'll fix it up somehow, even if Mic doesn't come to London.'

'I don't think she will come back.'

'Why?'

'She said she couldn't stand London.'

'Charming.'

'She's mad. But she's always like that, she never likes the place she's in.'

'Except Paris. Paris is perfect, according to her.'

'By the end of the winter she's grumbling about Paris, and hating it. When I saw her last she said she loathed Paris and her friends were all too boring for words.' He imitated her voice, ' "I shall expire with boredom. I am surrounded by the fourth-rate.".'

We chuckled. 'By the time that girl gets to University she'll be so pretentious she'll turn the stomach.' We sat in silence, considering Mic.

'I wonder what her future will be.'

'Stormy.' Joël yawned. 'At least she makes one speculate about her future. Not many could boast of that.'

My father appeared in a doorway. 'There you are. Tea. Then we must be off.' Stephen refused to leave the car, and therefore had no tea, a fact we all regretted later as we crawled into London delayed by traffic.

On Easter Monday I took Joël sight-seeing; it wasn't a very successful day, because we were both off-colour. I was depressed because he had to leave next morning; I had hoped to persuade him to stay. He said he had promised his parents, and that was it. It was only when we sat on a bench on the Embankment that our sour moods faded. The tide was high and the water yellow in the late afternoon sun.

'The Thames is beautiful. The banks aren't smelly like they are in Paris. Every tramp and dog in Paris pees on the Quais.'

'But people still fish in the Seine, don't they? There

137

are no fish in the Thames round London, though it's said they're coming back.'

'I've never seen anyone catch anything.' Joël stretched his legs out in front of him; not far away Big Ben chimed six. He yawned, and I caught it.

'We must get home. Mum's preparing a festive dinner, she said.'

'Your parents have been truly kind to me.'

'They like you.'

We walked to the tube station hand in hand. The train was crowded; our carriage was full of a party of German school-children. At the next station more people got in, and we were squashed up together. Joël put his arms round me, one hand holding on to the strut behind me. The other hand lay against my waist, a warm electrified pressure. I felt overwhelmed with tenderness towards him, and leant against his shoulder. He tightened his arm, and put his chin against my hair. We stayed in this position until we reached our station, even though by then the carriage was half empty.

Joël was hitchhiking down to Dover, so the next morning early we took a tube to the East End so that he could be on the main road he needed. Joël liked the sound of Stepney Green so we got out there.

'It isn't very green,' he said. We laughed ourselves silly over this, leaning back against the dirty tiled wall outside the station. It helped delay the moment when he had to start thumbing a lift. In the event he never started because a large lorry drew up beside us at the lights and I noticed it had a Dover address written on the side. We shouted at the co-driver, he opened the cab door, and Joël was gone when the lights changed. It was so quick I was still rolling up my used train ticket in my fingers when I returned to buy another.

'Clapham South.'

'Cheer up, girlie.' I looked up in surprise, unaware that my face reflected my feelings to that extent. Lonely, with a sense that part of me was missing, I went down and waited for a train. The carriage I got into was empty, and smelt acrid. I opened a window, but the cold air coming in from the dirty tunnel did nothing to freshen the carriage. I began to feel cold, but continued to sit in the stale draught. In my mind I started to write a letter to Joël; as soon as I got home I went up to my room and wrote it. Our correspondence was the backbone of my life through spring and summer until August came, and I returned to France.

9

I arrived at Tréguinec on the local bus. I had not expected to be met, because I hadn't specified which of the afternoon buses I would be on. Joël had not arrived in Tréguinec yet, and Mic was unlikely to bestir herself to meet a bus on the off-chance. In the event, I was glad no one was there. When I jumped off the bus, and dragged my case after me, I found to my surprise I was shaking. Tréguinec was so full of memories, and returning there made them rush to the surface again. I stood and looked at the bay; it was a cool, cloudy day, and the beach was not full. It wasn't a particularly beautiful bay, nor was there anything striking about the hinterland. The cliffs were less tall than I remembered them, the beach less long; it was a plain, everyday sort of place and I loved it. Down on the beach the priest was playing volleyball with his orphans, shouting instructions. His voice came up clearly.

I turned and started to walk up the hill to the Menards' cottages, carrying my case in short bursts. I thought about last summer, and the anguish I had felt about Antoine, and how something real had pushed that infatuation out of my heart. Because of my thoughts and the weight of my case, my head was bent down, and I jumped with surprise when a voice close by me said,

'Mon dieu, mon dieu! La petite Anglaise!'

It was Jean. He opened his arms with a great roar of welcome, and kissed me on both cheeks. He made so much noise that one or two of the orphans looked up from their game on the beach. He was wearing, as usual, an old tattered T-shirt, this time with *'J'aime la Bardot'* written across the front. His jeans were anchored round his waist with one of those thick elasticated stripey cords with a hook at each end. He insisted on carrying my case up to the Menards' for me. Once the great welcome was over he seemed shy.

'So you've come back to see your old friends?'

'Yes.'

'Mic isn't much of a friend not to come and meet you.'

'She didn't know which bus I was going to catch.'

'All the same.' He puffed a bit; he was fatter, or at least fatter than I remembered him to be.

'How's everything, Jean?'

'Ah, the world ticks by. More foreigners here this summer. Luckily they don't stay long, just pass through.' He sighed. I thought he looked sadder, less at peace with himself. I remembered him as being a man entirely content and relaxed.

'And your family?'

He shook his head up and down like a horse. 'My wife is fine. But my daughter Laure—what a disappointment.' He sighed again, and just as I was about to ask him why, he burst out, 'She ran away with a sailor. Just like that. *Poum.*' He drew an arc in the air with his free hand. 'Gone.'

I was surprised. Laure had not looked at all the sort of girl to do a bunk with a sailor. When I met her she was scrubbed and shiny, and yet sweaty; not at all attractive. Either she'd improved, or the sailor liked her that way.

'We thought she was young, innocent, carefully brought up to behave correctly. Now all I know for certain is that she is young.'

Perhaps Laure had got up to all sorts of activities in

secret, long before she eloped. Her face had fooled everyone, if that was so. But we all live immensely secret lives, after all; it seemed Joël and I told each other everything, yet I kept a great deal hidden in spite of myself, and so did he.

We were at the gate; Jean stopped, and lowered my case just inside the gate without stepping inside himself. It was as if he thought himself unfit or unwelcome on Menard ground. I thanked him warmly, and shook his hand. As I did so I heard Madame Menard calling my name. She appeared between the cottages; Jean beetled off, unremarked by her. I didn't like her for ignoring him.

Madame Menard was not precisely as I remembered her. It was difficult to pin down why; I realized she had dyed her hair, but that was only part of the difference. Mic appeared too, dressed in black trousers, black jersey and a black beret. Madame eyed her crossly.

'Ciao.' Mic's tone was casual, but she looked pleased to see me. 'Your hair's grown longer. Same room.' She jerked her head at the window, and together we lugged my case up the noisy wooden stairs.

'What the hell have you got in here?'

'Books. I must do some work.'

The smell of the cottage was the same; an unforgettable combination of Gauloises and garlic, calor gas, dried sea salt, oak furniture, and Ambre-Solaire. Sand and seashells still lay thick on the floors. I had the same Breton cupboard bed to sleep in. It was good to be back.

Mic said, making an effort to speak slowly, 'When you've unpacked we'll go down to the café.'

'Let's go straight away. I can't be bothered to unpack now.' I rattled this off.

'Your French has improved.' Mic was as unenthusiastic as ever about other people's achievements. 'I've nearly forgotten my English.'

'You should have come to stay.'

'I had to go to Germany to practise my German.'

'How was it?'

'Heavy going.'

'I'll just put on my jeans.'

Mic lay down on the bed while I rooted in my case. After a pause she said, 'I'm bored at Tréguinec this summer. There's nothing to do, and no one interesting to talk to. I'm bored, bored, bored.'

There didn't seem to be a good answer to this, so I took out a parcel and tossed it to her. 'For you.' It landed with a bump on her stomach. She opened it languidly, still lying down. It was a black leather belt with a heart-shaped brass buckle. She leapt off the bed and put it on, extremely pleased, her languid air gone. She pranced all the way down to the café, her thin body looking like a black cat.

'Already here,' said Jean to me.

'My mother's a drag,' said Mic. 'I can't bear to be in the same place as her any longer than is strictly necessary.'

Jean looked tired and disapproving, but said nothing. We started to play ping-pong, and after a few minutes he came and sat near us. We chattered spasmodically.

'Your French has improved,' he said to me. 'It was good last year, but now it's perfect.'

'That's what I said.' Mic caught me off my guard, and shot a smash into the corner. As I retrieved the ball I decided not to say what I had nearly said, that I had been writing letters in French all the year.

'I've been working hard at it. I want to go to University to study French.'

'I thought you wanted to be an actress,' said Jean.

'I can still take it up afterwards if I want to.'

Jean was engrossed in opening a packet of chewing gum. He put all five pillows of gum in his mouth in quick succession.

'I've given up smoking,' he said gloomily, 'and all I do is eat le chewing gum.'

'Why give it up?' said Mic. 'You might just as well die of nicotine poisoning as old age.'

'The doctor said it was imperative, or I would cough myself to death.' Poor Jean had his troubles. I smiled at him, and he tweaked my ear. 'Nice to see you, *petite Anglaise*.'

A crowd of noisy French came in at that moment, and he went off to serve them.

'New people,' muttered Mic to me under her breath. 'They've just built a villa somewhere nearby, and they're awful. The worst sort of Parisien.'

They looked all right to me, but I didn't argue with her.

'Tréguinec is getting spoilt by all these people.' She tossed her bat on the table. 'I'm fed up with this game. Let's go.' Out she went. Mic was obviously in a difficult mood, and I was glad to think Joël was due to arrive soon. His last letter had been unclear about precisely which day; their departure from Paris hitched in with meeting some South American cousin who Joël said was *fort amusant*.

I caught Mic up and we strolled along the beach. 'Who's here in Tréguinec?' I asked her. The strong cool wind had driven most people off the beach by now. Mic looked at me slyly.

'Antoine's here, if that's what you mean.'

'Oh, is he?'

'Oh, is he?' she mocked. 'You don't fool me. Last summer you couldn't take your eyes off him.'

Ah, but I do fool you Mic dear, but not in the way you think.

'Well, he's very good-looking. Why shouldn't I look at him?'

'Anyway, he's here. Not that you'll see much of him, he's working on some book. He hardly comes to the beach at all.'

I felt no wrench in the pit of the stomach as we talked about him; but I did feel shy of meeting him.

145

'By the way, do you remember I said last summer that his marriage didn't look very healthy to me?'

'Um.' I remembered Mic's remarks perfectly.

'I was nearer the truth than you thought. Marie has left him.' Mic said this rather gloatingly.

'Don't be horrid about it.'

'What do you mean, horrid . . .'

'It's sad when a marriage breaks up.'

'Ooh la la. We *have* become mature and sensible.'

'Oh, shut up.' Mic laughed.

'Apparently Marie went off to live by herself in Rome. It all sounded pretty smokey to me.'

I did not want to speculate about Antoine's troubles, so I didn't reply. We walked along in silence for a while, before I said, 'Who else is here?'

'The Jouberts haven't arrived yet.'

'I know. Jean said they hadn't.'

'Françoise de la Tour is here. Michelle and Marie-France Lamartine and their bunch. And a whole lot of strangers.'

'And the Baron?'

'He's in gaol of course.'

'I know that, but what's happening to his house?'

'I don't know precisely, but the rumour's going round that some Americans are buying it. That'll be the last straw.'

'You don't seem very fond of foreigners.'

'They're all a lot of stupid bums.'

Mic's prejudices are always whole-hearted. If it occurred to her I was in the bum category, she did not care. I liked her for it.

'What about the dolmen?'

She looked blank at first. 'Oh, the dolmen. Still in pieces. No one seems to be doing anything about it. What does it matter anyway, there are enough bally dolmens in Brittany.'

We were near the short cut up to the Menards' cottages. I'd had enough of Mic. 'I'm going to unpack.' I shot off up the path. When I looked back from the top Mic had rolled up her black trousers and was swinging her feet through the sea; the way she kicked the waves showed her bad mood. She seemed better this year than last at hiding her good points.

Joël did not arrive the following day, nor was there any sign of him the day after. I began to wish that I had left London later myself. The weather stayed cool, and Mic was tiresome. Things were very quiet, and she was bored. The only friend we saw at length was Françoise, who joined Mic in a grouch about how tedious Tréguinec was becoming.

'I'm too old for this sort of holiday,' said Françoise. She was even more polished and elegant, and looked and talked as if she was adult. In fact, I suppose she was. She chatted to Madame Menard as much as she did to us. I was surprised when Madame said, after Françoise had left, 'That girl gives herself too many airs!' I remembered my father saying once that he felt threatened when he realized that someone he had considered a child was a child no longer. Perhaps Madame felt the same and was bitchy about Françoise for that reason.

We were eating supper in silence on my third evening in Tréguinec when there was a tapping on the window. There was Joël; his grin was the sun to me. Behind him were Marcel and Suzanne. I was about to jump up and rush to the door when I saw that the others were taking the Jouberts' arrival calmly. I sat down again. Mic had no idea Joël and I had written to each other, or that he had come to London to see me. My hands were shaking.

Suzanne danced in front, shouting, *'Nous voilà, nous voilà!'*

'We can see,' said Mic. Now we all rose from the table and shook hands and kissed cheeks all round. Joël kissed my cheeks in the same manner he had kissed Mic's but he whispered a word as he did so which I

147

didn't catch. His hands were shaking too. His lips felt slightly bristly.

'But how you've grown!' Madame Menard exclaimed at him. 'Look at our big boy. Perhaps I should say man.' She looked at him coyly: an embarrassing look, which left a small silence behind it. Joël's tall body, vivid face and red hair filled the room.

'We came down in our new car,' said Marcel. A conversation about it developed between him and the boys. Chairs were pulled up to the table for the new arrivals—they had eaten earlier. Joël pushed his chair in beside mine; we exchanged a quick glance. Mic looked at us with a sudden shut expression. She could be perceptive enough about other people when it pleased her; and especially when she could scent a close relationship. Joël and I were such good friends now that we could take any amount of her teasing, I reflected; and that would annoy her.

'Well, Mic, how did your exams go?' asked Joël.

'Failed.'

'Bad luck.'

'Not bad luck at all,' started Madame. 'She fully deserved to fail . . .'

'Maman, please.' Mic's despairing tone was unusual, and her mother shut up.

'We stayed on in Paris to see Uncle Joël,' said Suzanne. 'He took all of us to the Tour d'Argent for lunch yesterday. He's terribly rich now.'

'He must be,' said Madame, 'to take the Joubert tribe to a restaurant like that.' After a pause she asked Joël, 'Where does he fit into your family?'

'He's my mother's eldest brother.'

'Ah, I remember now.'

'He's made a fortune in South America,' said Suzanne. She was excited by her uncle's wealth. 'He gave Joël a beautiful watch, inscribed *"De Joël à Joël"*.'

'Let's see it,' said Mic at once.

'I left it in Paris,' said Joël.

'What did he give you, Suzie?'

'The girls got pearl brooches.'

'All the same?'

'Yes.' She sounded less enthusiastic.

'I wish we had a rich uncle,' said Angélique. 'There's no one rich in our family at all, is there, Maman?'

'I think these expensive presents are vulgar,' said Mic.

'You're just jealous,' said Suzanne.

'I'm not at all.'

To give Mic her due, I don't think she was. Suzanne glared at her.

'You're a born spoil-sport, Mic,' she said bitterly.

'I'm just a realist.'

'Oh ho ho,' scoffed Madame Menard.

Under cover of this conversation, Joël had whispered, 'How are you?'

'I couldn't wait for you to arrive.'

'I couldn't wait to come.'

He ran his finger lightly up and down the back of my hand, which was lying on my knee. His finger felt extra alive. 'I'll meet you tomorrow at the café at ten o'clock. Come alone if you can get away.' We rejoined the general conversation. After a while Joël stood up.

'Come on, kids. We must get back. We said we'd only be half an hour.'

'You really have grown,' said Madame again.

'For God's sake, Maman. We all know what a great big piece of beef Joël's grown into but don't keep reminding us.' Mic had her ear taken by Joël, but neither was annoyed. 'Let go, you brute.'

After they had gone, we played cards inattentively, and soon after went to bed. Mic livened up then, and did exercises round the bedroom which she said were based on Yoga. I lay in bed trying to ignore her, but she kept on talking, saying things like,

'Let us say you could cut a man in half as you can a worm, and each bit would grow into a new man. What sort of memories would the new man have of his past existence?'

I did not answer, and she launched into another equally pointless and tortured speculation.

'The trouble with you, Mary, is that you have no intellectual curiosity.'

'Those ideas are so tedious.'

Mic sighed, and did a protracted handstand against the Breton *armoire*. She panted out some remark about Joël while upside down.

'What?'

She righted herself. 'I said, Joël's improved. In fact he's got quite good-looking.' Her hair hung in a curtain over her face, obscuring her expression. 'Don't you agree, Mary?' Her voice told me nothing.

'Yes.'

'In a year or two, the star attraction in Tréguinec won't be Antoine, it'll be Joël.' She tossed back her hair, revealing wicked eyes. 'A fact I think you've already grasped, clever Mary Meredith.' She went into her room which joined mine. I didn't answer. In a way, she had a point. I heard her rattling and chattering about for some time.

'Aren't you going to bed?'

'No. The best time of each day is from midnight till three. It's a marvellous, intense period. One should be awake.'

'Doesn't your mother object?'

'I do what I please in my own room.' Mic's voice last year saying '*Je suis égoiste, moi*' came clearly back to me. It impressed me then, her attitudinizing. I felt uneasy now. Mic appeared in the doorway in bra and pants.

'You'll become a prig, Mary. Watch out.'

'I will not.'

She laughed. 'The English are all prigs.'

'Don't be ridiculous.'

She threw herself on the bed, still laughing. I wanted to get up and punch her, but I resisted the temptation. She loved a fight.

Next morning I slipped down to the café without Mic, who was still in bed despite Madame's raucous yells up the stairs. Joël was there, talking to Jean about the Côtes du Nord Cycling Championship. The entrants were riding through Tréguinec that week. Jean was a great enthusiast and always closed the café during the race. Not that it was closed for long; the cyclists had shot through in a bunch last year, leaving disappointed crowds. I thought it was a dull sport. I stood near Joël, and he took my hand.

Jean looked cheerful this morning. He stopped talking about cycling when he saw me, and held up a letter.

'From Laure.'

'What does she say? Joël, Laure has run away with a sailor.'

'No!'

'She says she's very happy, that the man is *bon type*, and that we must forgive her.' He poked his thick finger at the letter, which consisted of a page of careful writing.

'Do you forgive her?'

'Forgive, what does the word mean?' Jean shrugged, his shoulders and whole back bunching up expressively. 'To me, forgiveness doesn't exist. People do things which hurt you, and after a while you forget. Perhaps you come to understand why they did it. But forgiveness—that's not an emotion I feel.'

'So you won't see her again.'

'What do you mean? Of course we will see her, and meet the *bon type*. What else can we do? She's our only child, and we love her.' Jean looked quite annoyed with me.

'Some people would call that forgiveness,' said Joël.

'Well, I don't. Forgiveness is what the priests go on about, it's not for me.' Then with his usual quick change of mood, he pinched my cheek and winked at Joël.

'*La petite Anglaise* becomes very pretty, doesn't she, eh?'

'Very pretty,' said Joël. I felt a blush creep up my face, and couldn't meet his bright eyes.

'You are modest, my little chick,' said Jean. 'If you were Mic or Françoise, you'd know your physical value to the last inch.' He sighed, patted my head, and retreated on to his high stool behind the bar. 'French girls. Bah.'

'Let's go,' said Joël softly. We left Jean still muttering about French girls.

'I thought we might walk round the point, and bathe somewhere off the cliffs. We can go over the Baron's beach; the place is empty, Jean says.'

'It might be sold to Americans.'

'So I heard.'

'Mic's very angry about all the foreign tourists finding Tréguinec.'

'Mic is always angry about something. It's a disease with her. Anyway, *elle est très poseuse.*'

There was a pause before I said, 'So are all girls.'

'You don't pose.'

'Yes, I do.'

'As Jean says, you're natural.'

"You could say that's my pose, natural modest little me.' I felt a desire to blacken myself a little in his eyes. He was frowning, staring ahead as we walked down the beach towards the rocky point.

'But you don't think about the effect you're making all the time, the way Mic does.'

'No, I agree. I'm too lazy.'

'No one's lazier than Mic.'

'*Touché.*' I laughed, and Joël laughed a little too, unwillingly. He kicked a stone along, looking carefully away from me. He obviously did not like having his picture of me altered. I was doubtless wrong about some of his character too. After all we did not, could not, never would be able to know all there was to know about each other. It struck me forcibly in that moment that it would be dreadful to know everything about another human being. There would be no mystery or ambiguity.

'Mystery is important.'

'What did you say?'

'I was just muttering aloud.'

'Something about mystery.'

Reluctantly I said, 'I was thinking that it would be dreadful if there was no mystery about other people. If you knew everything about another person, you'd always know why they did things. There'd be no surprise.'

He turned to look at me again. 'You can still have perfect understanding without knowing everything, I think.'

'In special cases.'

As if the conversation was too heavy for this hot fine day, we started to run and jump along the sands.

The Baron's beach had an occupied air. The sand was full of footprints high above the tide mark, and already two families had settled themselves near rocks. The boat-house had been badly knocked about by vandals; one door hung open crookedly. It was quite empty. The Baron's house was all shuttered up, though Joël had been told that a caretaker lived in the back of it. It was exactly the same property as before, but the fascination was gone. Last summer, and our giggles as we crept along through the hedge into the Baron's garden, seemed another life. We were already, as Joël had remarked, completely different people.

We reached a rocky inlet with a small jetty, where a few fishing boats were moored. Except for an old Breton mending a net, there was no one there. We decided to swim off the jetty; the clear green water slurped invitingly against the rough granite walls. As we undressed the old fisherman watched us morosely; he rolled up the net, left it piled against some crabpots, and limped off up the cliff path.

I felt shy in my bathing suit, shy and exposed. My skin was still fairly white, despite spasmodic sunbath-

153

ing in the back garden at home. Somehow as we walked down towards the water Joël and I seemed all body. I dived straight in, and Joël followed, chasing me under water. We swam out to a blue fishing boat and tried to climb into it. This is notoriously difficult, and the boat was tall-sided into the bargain. We clambered, slipped back again, fell into the water with a splash and laughed at our efforts. At last Joël managed to get up into the boat, and dragged me after him. I got stuck, half way in, my legs kicking uselessly. Joël gave a heave and we both rolled giggling into the bottom of the boat. Still laughing, I began to untangle myself.

'We are silly.'

'Mary.'

Joël had stopped laughing. His face was covered with rivulets of seawater, and his eyelashes were separated into spikes; his hair, like mine, stuck wet to his head. He leaned his face close to mine, and I heard his quick breaths before he kissed me. His lips were cool, salty and wet, and he pressed them against mine, quite still. I am sure this was his first kiss, though I never asked him. After all, it was only my second.

He moved his mouth up and kissed my eye. I leant my face into his shoulder, and heard laughter. Up above us on the cliffs some children were watching us; I saw them pointing and sniggering. Joël had not heard them; he kissed my neck and shoulder, and tightened his arm round my waist.

'Look out.' I moved from Joël and pretended to look for something in the boat. 'Little blighters. Are they part of our group?'

Joël glared up at them until they moved on. 'I don't think so, but they're kids we often see around. *Fiche le camp.*'

There was a splash as he dived off the boat and swam furiously back towards the jetty. His arms went round like windmills and his heels flashed. I stayed on the boat for a while, conscious that our relationship had reached a turning point. I was even filled with an

154

irrational annoyance that Joël had forced the issue. I hoped the children would not gossip; it would be such a bad beginning if everyone heard we had been seen kissing in a boat.

Something cold and wet landed on my stomach. I sat up with a squeak; it was only a piece of frondy green seaweed. I looked over the side of the boat, and Joël grinned wickedly at me, his eyes as green as the sea he was in. Having thrown the weed back at him, I dived in and raced him to the jetty.

When we returned to the main beach it was after noon, and a large crowd had settled on the sands. The Menards, Jouberts and their gang seemed vast this morning, and their chatter was like a monkey house, the parents more noisy even than their offspring. Monsieur Joubert had a bottle of San Raphaël which he was pouring into picnic mugs and handing round. I had hardly noticed what he looked like the summer before; now I looked at him with interest, and saw how like him Joël was. He gave me a quick smile when he offered me some *apéritif,* and I felt his eyes on me several times after that. Joël's mother, when I shook hands with her, gave me an unenthusiastic smile, and hardly met my eyes.

'Thank you for being so kind to my son in London.' She made it seem we had performed an unpleasant duty rather well.

'We loved having him.'

She inclined her head, and smiled again. She was wearing a particularly fine old crucifix round her neck, and I remembered Joël saying that his mother took her religion seriously. She was plump, and the crucifix snuggled in the dip between her breasts. I'm not a Roman Catholic, a fact she no doubt knew.

Everyone grew mildly tiddly on the San Raphaël; the bottle was finished, and Monsieur Joubert stuck it neck down in the sand. We used it as a target and threw pebbles unsuccessfully at it. Engrossed in this game, I was unaware at first that Antoine had arrived.

'Alas, too late,' said Monsieur Joubert, dramatically indicating the empty bottle.

'I don't drink at midday when I'm working.' Antoine's voice made me jump. I could not help feeling tense, particularly when he reached me in the round of handshakes.

'Nice to see you at Tréguinec again,' he said, and passed on before I could mumble a reply. Joël threw a pebble at the bottle, and hit it with a hard clang.

Before we all left the beach for lunch, Antoine sat himself down in my line of vision and so I had an opportunity of looking at him more carefully. He was talking to Joël's father earnestly about something. He looked much older than I remembered, and his face was baggy round the mouth. His blue eyes did not seem as intense in colour, perhaps because this year he was not sun-tanned, but sallow. I realized that one of the things that had fed my infatuation was the contrast of blue eyes with brown skin, a simple fact of great visual attraction. His fixed, dead expression, and the air of exhaustion and depression he gave out, were disturbing. It didn't seem possible that a man could change so much in one year. But his wife had left him; I had forgotten that.

'You're working far too hard, then,' I heard Monsieur Joubert say. 'Nobody can keep up a pace like that.'

'I have to submit the book at the end of August. I've no choice.'

'Get an extension.'

'I've had two already. The publishers mean business this time.' He sounded gloomy. 'I finished all the research last year. Just couldn't get down to writing the book.'

'Research is pleasure, but writing a book about it is a painful process.'

'Too true.' He kneaded his forehead.

'All the same, take a few days off.'

Antoine smiled in the way people do when they think you've made a kind but pointless suggestion. He caught me looking at him, and swivelled his eyes away.

'I mean it. Come on a picnic with us this Sunday.'

'Perhaps, perhaps.' He got up, yawned and stretched.

'No excuses, we will make you. It's foolish to drive your brain too hard, you'll break down.' But Antoine left without finally agreeing. Monsieur Joubert said in an audible undertone to his wife, 'Poor man, he's obviously had a bad year. He looks ill.'

If anyone had told me the summer before that my feelings for Antoine, and Antoine himself, would have changed so much, I could not have believed them. I sat in a dream, thinking about Antoine, and Joël, and the oddness of it all. Not for long, because a quick cool hand inserted some sand-hoppers into my bathing suit and I had the pleasure of sorting myself out before Joël and I chased Mic until she screamed for mercy.

During that week I discovered how sensible the French are about a teenage relationship. Joël and I were treated as a foregone conclusion; no one remarked on our always being together; in fact everyone, including Mic, treated us as if we were an old married couple. I thought Mic would tease us, but she lost interest. She wasn't jealous of Joël. So we were taken as close friends, nothing special or romantic about us. As a result we did not behave romantically, and it was very comfortable, very sensible, very French. The real romance was something you kept hidden. I was very happy; I could hardly believe my luck.

'This time,' said Joël, 'we're going to show you a bit of Brittany. Staying on the beach all day gets tedious.' We were lying in the sun.

'I'd like to go to Carnac,' I said. 'It sounds a fascinating place.'

'It's a longish way. Perhaps we could persuade my father to drive us. Or Mic's.'

'I'm not coming. I've been to Carnac once, and once is enough.' Mic was sitting in her black outfit looking very hot. She was glued to Françoise's copy of *Elle;* they both read it from cover to cover each week.

'Why don't you take those clothes off? You look cooked.'

She took her attention off *Elle* long enough to look at me coldly and say, 'I will always sacrifice comfort for effect.'

I believed her.

'I was in a black mood this morning.' She went back to *Elle*.

There was a silence as we gathered energy to return to the former discussion.

'I'd quite like to see Carnac,' said Françoise.

'We'll go.' Joël yawned.

'What happened to that Englishman, Thomas something? He was always going on about Carnac. Did he write his book?'

'I don't think it's published yet. I spoke to him on the telephone once and he said he'd just got married. I haven't heard from him or seen him since.'

'Being married keeps you busy,' said Françoise. Mic giggled. She and Françoise often had lengthy conversations in undertones punctuated by much snickering and giggling. I noticed though that Françoise would stop whenever there was an adult nearby.

There was a tearing sound as Mic carelessly turned a page. 'Mind my magazine,' said Françoise. She stretched and sighed heavily. *'Mon dieu,* I'm bored at Tréguinec.'

'I thought you were going to spend this summer in the south of France,' I said. 'I remember you saying last year that you wouldn't be here this summer.'

'My sister's having a baby, so they've not taken their villa this year. The baby is due any day now.' She looked unimpressed.

'You'll be an aunt,' said Mic. '*Tante* Françoise. What a laugh. Ah, *tante* Françoise, wipe up this sick would you. *Tante* Françoise, be careful, you're holding the baby upside down.'

'*Tais-toi!*'

Finally, Mic did.

'How old's your sister?' I asked.

'Nineteen.'

'God.' In three years' time I could be married and have my first baby. Objectively it was an appalling prospect. The idea of getting married young had never occurred to me. Even Joël had not changed that. I could feel him listening, lying still with his eyes closed.

'That's not so young.' Françoise was defensive. 'In France it's common to marry at eighteen, and start your family.'

'I'd hate to tie myself down so young.'

'So should I,' said Mic. 'I want to knock about the world living a life rich in experience until I'm at least twenty-five. Then, renowned as a *femme fatale,* I will catch my millionaire.'

'You make me sick,' said Joël.

'She's not serious,' I said.

'She is.'

Mic laughed, tossed *Elle* aside, and lay back in the sand, shutting her eyes. The black belt I had given her lay on her flat stomach, the buckle flashing in the sun. Not far off I saw a young man watching us intently. His expression was like that on a little boy's face looking in a toyshop window; then he saw me looking at him and glanced away, pretending indifference. I looked at my companions: they were three attractive young people, and it was no wonder they drew the eye.

With a sudden easy movement, Joël stood up. He towered above us against the blue sky.

'You've grown so tall,' Françoise said pensively.

'Come on. We're all getting lazy.' He pulled me to my feet and we started to run down the beach. The other two did not follow.

The Jouberts had a battered old canoe which I had not seen the year before. It had been mended and put back into use, and was the favourite activity of the moment. It lived up behind Jean's café. We dragged it down to the water's edge on its trailer of old pram-wheels, and launched it. The inside held two people comfortably and smelt of tar. Joël sat behind me and wedged his feet against my back before we paddled off. The paddles were made of old ping-pong bats hammered to the end of poles. We progressed slowly across the bay. My arms got tired after a while so I leant back against Joël's horny knees and let him do most of the work. Later he stopped his efforts too, and we drifted along some way out.

'No dangerous currents here?'

'No.'

The sea undulated. We sat in a thinking silence, which at length Joël broke.

'Mic makes me angry.'

'Don't show it, because she enjoys needling you.'

'To hell with her. I see her sometimes in Paris; she always goes to a certain pavement café with her gang and there they sit for an hour or so after school. She always makes a point of giggling as you walk past and saying something about you to her companions which they all laugh at. Charming girl really.'

'I long to see Paris. I'll come and stay with you some time.'

'Come for Christmas. We spend a week in Paris and then we go skiing. You could come with us.'

It was such a good prospect it almost hurt.

'Oh, Joël. Yes. I'll come if my parents let me. I'm sure they will if they can afford it.' I would ask for the trip as my Christmas present, I would save up the extra. Somehow I would get to Paris that Christmas. I tried to turn round in the boat and it almost capsized.

'For goodness' sake sit still.'

'The future's so exciting.'

'Row. That'll get rid of your bounce.' So we rowed

energetically for a spell, and stopped again, this time heading back to Tréguinec.

'Do you remember a conversation we had in London about my going on the stage?'

'Clearly.' His tone was noncommittal.

'You said my temperament was unsuitable, remember?'

'I was talking rubbish.'

'But I was just going to say I thought you were probably right.'

'I had no business to say what I did. I was being very pompous. If it's what you long to do, then you must do it to fulfil something in yourself. People must not interfere in these matters.'

'Well, I'm not sure any more it's what I want to do.'

'I thought you were dead set on it.'

'Now I know I'm good my attitude's changed. I don't know.'

'You mustn't listen to what I say.'

'How can I help it? What you say matters to me.'

'I'm sorry I discouraged you.'

'Joël, perhaps I would have changed my mind in time anyway. I haven't really changed it yet, either; I just know that I must go to university first and study something for its own sake, probably French, maybe archaeology. Then after that I can decide.'

There was a pause; Joël trailed his hand in the sea, making the canoe veer slightly. Then he said, 'We'll definitely go to Carnac while you're here. You and I will go by bus if no one will drive us. We can camp there and come back next day.'

We saw a figure waving a towel at us from the beach. A faint yodel reached us. The beach was almost empty.

'It must be lunchtime.'

'Or later.'

'Oh, dear.'

We paddled quickly, and saw Suzanne disappear up

161

the beach when she realized we were returning. We dragged the canoe out of the sea; we were alone on the beach. Cooking smells wafted down.

'*A toute à l'heure.*' Joël shouldered the paddles, and leaned forward and kissed my forehead. We went off in opposite directions. Life was very good.

10

The Sunday picnic took place, and Antoine came, persuaded by Monsieur Joubert. Cars and people collected outside the Menards. Antoine smiled and chatted, but his eyes were sad, and he looked like someone making the best of things. Perhaps he had loved his wife very much and still could not bear life without her. He brought his car, and Mic, Joël and I and little Dominique travelled with him. Mic sat in front with Antoine. Joël and I took turns to read *Tintin* to Dominique.

As we rounded a headland, Antoine jabbed at a button and his radio blared out. He adjusted it, and the car was full of pleasant French pop. We let *Tintin* ride for a bit, and all sat back and wallowed in the music, the sun pouring through the open sun-roof.

There's always something special about driving along in sunshine with music thick around you; it's a sure recipe for happiness, mindless physical happiness. I was happy anyway; now I felt an almost aching joy. A pretty swelling tune started, and it seemed of the greatest beauty, though I expect in another mood I would have found it insipid.

Even then, in my excess of emotion, I wondered whether moments of happiness like this happened very often; whether it was possible, so early in my life, to feel a peak of happiness I could not exceed. Just at that point of thought, the tune changed again, and without a break the familiar eerie introduction of *Ne me quitte pas* began.

Mic swung her feet up on the dashboard. 'Marvellous.'

Though it's not a song one joins in with, this time all of us in the car except Dominique sang it quietly, almost to ourselves, in time to the recorded singer's voice. It sounded oddly as if we were taking part in a rite. When it was over the atmosphere in the car had changed; Antoine pressed the button gently and there was silence.

'After that, all is bathos,' said Antoine with deliberate melodrama. He smacked Mic's feet down from the dashboard.

There are days in your life when everything you do, see, feel or touch is heightened. That Sunday was one of those days with me. It surprised me to learn that Joël had a bad headache and was not enjoying himself; my mood was invincible despite this.

We picnicked at the very end of a headland, a long low out-crop of hillocky grass with beautiful rounded red rocks surrounding the grass and going into the sea like the backs of red elephants. The sand between the rocks was very coarse, as if it had been only recently ground up by waves and wind. It was painful to walk on for any distance. We sat on the grass in a true dell, which was full of pink and blue thrift and white campion. One pink flower grew alone on top of a rock near me; how it lived I could not see. I remember it as clearly as I remember everything about that day.

A Joubert-organized picnic was different from a Menard one; there was a large plastic container full of delicious croquettes and beignets of this and that which Madame Joubert had made. When you bit into one you never knew what your tongue would find; rice and cheese, aubergine, sausage, rice and meat, or chicken, potato, fish. Madame Joubert must have spent the whole of Saturday baking. I think she was the type

164

of woman my father described as a willing sacrifice on the domestic altar. My mother was an unwilling one.

As we ate, small butterflies with wings of blue on one side, creamy white on the other, fluttered near us. Seagulls screeched noisily and continuously about half a mile away, where fishermen had thrown something they liked on the rocks. Before our picnic was over, they finished whatever it was, and silence descended as the birds drifted away, planing in the air.

Joël slept most of the afternoon in the sun; when it was time to leave, he said his headache was much worse.

'If you sleep in the sun, what can you expect?' said his mother brusquely. The baby was playing up by this time, and her temper was short.

Joël shrugged, but I noticed he was pale, and his hands felt clammy. We returned as we had come in Antoine's car, this time without Dominique, who was keen on plaguing his mother too. Joël flopped in the back seat, saying nothing. I still felt happy and suntoasted, so I leaned forward and talked to Mic. Antoine must have noticed Joël's face in the driving mirror, because he said suddenly, slowing down, 'Do you want to be sick, Joël? You look bad. Shall I stop?'

'No, no. I don't feel very sick.'

'You look it.'

'I feel shivery. My head hurts.' He held the back of his head and neck. 'I think I've probably got a temperature.'

I put my hand on Joël's forehead and it felt very hot. Yet he shivered, and wrapped a beach towel round his shoulders to keep himself warm.

Antoine frowned. 'You've clearly got a fever of some sort.' He had been driving fast anyway, but he speeded up by deciding to leave the pretty winding coast road and take the straighter inland road instead.

'I wonder what you've got.' I felt a spasm of fear, which passed at once.

Mic said, 'I expect you've got sunstroke. You did sleep in the sun, after all. It's been very hot.'

'Could be.' Joël was past caring, hunched up in his corner with his eyes shut. Mic chatted to Antoine, while I sat in the back willing Joël to have nothing worse than summer 'flu. It would be exceedingly annoying if he had something more serious and infectious as well, which would spoil our holiday together. Selfish though it was, I couldn't help feeling peeved with him for being ill. I remember feeling exactly the same annoyance with Stephen when he developed measles just before we were supposed to spend a week in Wales, and as a result none of us went.

Joël groaned suddenly and held his head. 'Aah.'

'What is it?'

'My whole head hurts so much.' He rocked himself about. 'Aah. Aai.' The groans of pain were involuntary; he hardly knew what he was doing. I put my arm round his shoulders, but he was beyond being comforted. I began to feel afraid; the spasm of fear which had crossed my mind earlier now returned and stayed put. Something was very wrong. My stomach started to ice over. I leaned forward and interrupted Antoine, who was telling Mic about a professor she hoped one day to work under.

'Antoine. He's really ill.' Antoine took a quick look at Joël and stopped the car.

'We'll lie him down on the back seat. You sit on Mic's knee.' But I managed to squeeze myself into the gap between the front and back seats, and sat on the floor beside Joël. I wrapped the towel round him. His pale drawn face was near mine, but he was unaware of me.

Antoine and Mic discussed the local doctors. The most hopeful possibility was that a Parisian doctor, Dupont, was on holiday in his villa on the edge of Tréguinec. Mic said she had seen his wife in the village a few days before.

We were nearly in Tréguinec. Antoine said to Mic, 'Do you know exactly where Dupont lives? I don't.'

'Yes.'

'Good. I think it's wisest to go straight there. We'll leave Mary behind at the Jouberts to tell them what's happened when they arrive. O.K.?'

Nothing was less O.K. to me than being left in Tréguinec to wait, but I could see there was no choice. I climbed out, miserable.

'Can't we leave a note?'

'We don't go past the Jouberts to get to the doctor's,' said Mic. She did not look at me.

'*Au revoir,* Joël. *A bientôt.*' He was curled up with his back towards me, and did not reply. I squeezed his shoulder, and they drove off. I walked down along the seafront to the Jouberts' battered villa, and sat down on the steps of Joël's caravan to wait. I found my hands were clenched with anxiety. No one came, and the sun was low in the sky now. By craning through the kitchen window, I could see the time was six thirty-five. I had been waiting at least half an hour. They had to come by seven, they just had to.

I went back to the caravan. I tried the door, even though I knew it was locked. Then I sat down on the step again. Beside me was a brick, which I kicked with my feet; under it was the key of the caravan. I let myself in.

The whole place was untidy and smelt male. I was reassured by the evidence of Joël everywhere; his books, his files, his familiar clothes. Tossed on the bed was his large red-and-white striped jersey. I picked it up and sniffed his own particular pleasant smell.

Pinned up above his work table, spread with books, was the notice, 'Hands off my pen, Marcel, or I'll grill you alive.' Also pinned up was a sort of printed motto, very tattered, which read,

'To know, to will, to dare, to be silent.' There were dog-eared photographs stuck behind a slat, one of Bob Dylan, one of Jacques Brel.

I felt chilly, so I put Joël's jersey on; it hung almost down to my knees. Joël's scent was very comforting. I looked at the motto again. I didn't see the point of it, to be honest. There's not much to be gained from being silent as a way of life, it seems to me.

I thought I heard a car stop, and ran from the caravan. But it was not the Jouberts' car; whoever it was drove on down the road. I could have cried from disappointment. I went to look at the time again; ten to seven. I leaned my face against the window and shut my eyes in desperation.

Just after seven the Jouberts' estate car drew up. It turned out that they were late because they had stopped to eat at a *crêperie*. As soon as the car arrived, Dominique sang out through the window,

'We've been eating pancakes! I ate three.'

'Two and a half.'

The sight of the family was such a relief to me I felt tears rise and trickle down my cheeks. I opened my mouth to speak, but nothing came out. At this moment Monsieur Joubert became aware of my face against the noisy background of his children. 'What's the matter, Mary? What's happened?'

'Joël collapsed in the car. Antoine's taken him to the doctor.'

'Which doctor?' He did not sound unduly impressed. I could not remember the doctor's name; my mind was a jelly in which facts had submerged.

'Which doctor?'

'What's the problem?' Madame struggled out of the car with Pish sleeping in her arms.

'It appears Joël's been taken ill. Which doctor, Mary?' He gripped my shoulder.

'The one who comes here on holiday from Paris. They went off to his villa to see if he was there.'

'Dupont.'

'Yes, yes.'

'How long ago was this?' Monsieur started to unpack the car in a leisurely way.

'I expect it's sunstroke,' said Madame, disappearing with Pish.

'It was an hour ago at least they dropped me off, so that I could wait here and tell you.'

'Oh, well, in that case they'll be back soon, I should think.' He fished about in the boot. I could feel myself going rigid; I had imagined we would drive off at once to the doctor's; I never expected this calm acceptance. It was the obvious and sensible approach, but I had an agonized feeling that every minute was important.

'We ought to go to the doctor's.'

'Don't worry, Antoine will bring Joël back here. What's the point of such a crowd of us bothering the doctor?'

'We must go. Joël's ill.' My words had no effect, though he smiled at me kindly. Madame returned to help carry things from the car. 'Please, Madame, Joël's really ill.' She came to my rescue.

'Marc, you must go. You can then bring Joël back yourself and save Antoine the trouble.'

There was a pause during which I dared not look at either of them. Then Monsieur Joubert said, 'Come on. We'll probably meet them on the way.' He shrugged. He clearly thought it was a fuss about nothing.

'Joël's had sunstroke before,' said Madame to me through the car window. 'He shouldn't have fallen asleep in the sun.'

'Perhaps it's not sunstroke.'

'What else could it be?' She smiled at me more sympathetically than she ever had before. Monsieur had gone into the villa to relieve himself, and I found I was gripping the sides of my seat as if this pressure would make the car go. At last we were off, and I sank back.

'I'm not sure where this fellow Dupont's villa is,' said Monsieur, and I realized my relief was short-lived. We circled about endlessly, trying a couple of the roads winding out of Tréguinec, before he could bring himself

169

to ask the way. I thought I would fall apart with frustration. By chance the man we asked knew the house; we came to a large square villa with blue shutters, very prim-looking, and inside the gate was Antoine's Renault.

'Well, they're still here.' Monsieur sounded surprised.

The sight of the Renault increased my sense of fear, though why I didn't know. There was no sign of anyone, and it was ages before an unfriendly woman answered the bell.

'What do you want?'

'Doctor Dupont lives here I believe . . .'

'He's very busy at the moment.' She started to shut the door; I was ready to rush at it. I heard Mic's voice inside the house somewhere. I almost shouted to her.

'My son has been taken ill and brought here by friends . . .' began Monsieur.

'Ah, *pardon*. Come in.' Her unfriendliness became kind exhaustion. She led us to a sun-room where we found Antoine and Mic. 'Please wait here.'

'Where on earth have you *been?*' burst out Mic.

'Poor Mary had to wait a long time for us because we stopped at a *crêperie*.'

'Where's Joël? What's happened?'

'Doctor Dupont's only just arrived himself, he was out fishing . . .'

Antoine interrupted the gabble. 'Marc, there was clearly something wrong with the boy. He was hardly conscious by the time Dupont arrived. He's got Joël on a couch in his study now.'

'What on earth's the matter with the boy?' Joubert was upset and angry.

'Dupont is still examining him.'

'Estelle is sure it's sunstroke. Joël's had it before, and he slept all afternoon in the sun.'

'I mentioned that to Dupont.'

'And?'

'He said nothing. Took very little notice of me.' Antoine knocked his sunglasses in the palm of his hand.

'Have you got a Gauloise, by the way? I always run out in a crisis. I need a smoke.'

"Sorry, Antoine, no luck.' Monsieur Joubert paced over to the window and back. I slumped on to the arm of a chair. I felt drained, empty, detached. My immediate anxiety had faded now I had reached the doctor's, but this did not give me any feeling of relief. I was numb.

After a silence, Antoine said, 'Look, would you mind if I left you all to it? I've got to get back. Now that you're here, Marc . . .'

'Of course, of course. You go.'

'I'd stay if I thought I was necessary . . .'

'No, no, we can manage. You go. You've got work to do.'

'That's right.' Antoine went to the door. 'Do you want to go back, Mic?'

'No, I'm staying.' He left.

A dreadful howling noise broke out in the corridor, and we all froze. The door pushed open and a Siamese cat came in and made the noise again. We started to laugh with relief.

'What a fiendish sound!'

The cat jumped on to my lap and crouched, asking to be patted on its back. Madame Dupont peered in, perhaps because she had heard us laughing, frowned, and disappeared again.

Monsieur Joubert threw himself on to a wicker sofa with a sigh. 'It's all a bit worrying. To be honest, I don't think he can have sunstroke. It's more likely to be a virus infection.'

'He said he had ear-ache,' said Mic. 'Bad ear-ache.'

Joubert cheered up. 'Well, he's had an ear infection before. That's more possible.' He thought about it. 'I used to have ear troubles myself.'

I heard a telephone ring faintly; it was picked up at once. Soon after, footsteps came down the corridor and a man appeared in a fisherman's jersey and sailcloth trousers. He stared in surprise at the changed occupants of the room.

'Doctor Dupont?' began Monsieur Joubert.

'Where's the boy's father gone?' Dupont glared at Mic. 'Who are all these people?'

'I'm the boy's father. I came as soon as I could.'

'Oh, I see. Yes, of course, I remember the other man explained.' He saw the cat on my lap, came across, took it firmly and put it out of the room, closing the door. When he turned round he said, his face grave,

'Your son's in a coma.' We stared at him appalled.

'From sunstroke, or what?' said Monsieur Joubert at last.

'Of course not. He hasn't got sunstroke.' He looked sternly at Mic and myself. 'Are these his sisters?'

'No. Friends.'

'Do you want them to go while I tell you about your son's condition?'

I willed Joël's father with my entire being not to banish us from the room. There was a pause, but when I looked at him I saw that he had hardly heard what the doctor had said. He waved his hand in an impatient gesture of permission.

'I am not positive,' said the doctor at last, 'but the signs point to meningitis.'

I did not know what meningitis was, but Monsieur's face was so horrorstruck I realized the disease was serious. My stomach began to ice over again. I did not move.

'Ah, *non.*'

'I'm not certain, as I said. But almost. An ambulance is on its way, and will take your son to the big hospital in Rennes, where he will be examined, and treated.' He and Monsieur sat down and the doctor started writing down details about Joël. Mic and I went to the windows and talked under cover of the question and answer behind us.

'Do you know what meningitis is?'

'Not precisely, I know it's a sort of brain fever, that's

all. *C'est très grave.*' Mic looked uneasy, as if she knew something more. After a pause she muttered, 'People die of it.'

Madame Dupont opened the door behind us and came in followed by the cat uttering its unearthly cries. She brought a tray of coffee, obviously under her husband's instructions. I must have drunk mine, but I don't remember doing it.

The cat suddenly ran up the curtain and got itself a perch on the pelmet. Madame Dupont shrieked, 'My new curtains! Ah, *c'est trop.*'

'Don't make so much noise. That boy is seriously ill.' The doctor spoke to his wife as if she was a child. 'I'll have that cat shot.'

The words 'seriously ill' said brusquely in that context undid me. I found tears running down my face even though inside I was still numb with shock. No one took any notice of me.

It seemed a long time later that Marc Joubert touched my shoulder. He looked pale. 'Would you like to come and sit beside Joël until the ambulance arrives?'

I nodded, but felt afraid. The doctor's wife, the cat and Mic were nowhere to be seen.

Joël was lying on a low couch in the next room. The doctor called Joubert away and I was left alone with him. He was very still, wrapped in a plaid rug. I sat down on a low chair near his head. I don't know how long I was alone with him in that peaceful room, time is so elastic. I remember it as a precious hour in which every minute made its presence felt. I had time to see the precise way his hair grew, that thick red hair. Joël had three crowns, and the hair whorled from each into conflicting hillocks of curls. The dense coppery colour appeared lighter at the roots. Hair curled into his ears, which had a dusting of sand inside. His ear-lobes were surprisingly large, and one had a neat brown birthmark on its tip. His freckles stood out on his pale face; they looked as if they had been carefully drawn in with a brush. His eyelashes were short and singed-looking. But no eyes, no lively green eyes. His lids never lifted. It was odd to think that beneath those lids I was looking at so closely lay, just through a thin film of flesh, those eyes.

His hands were square with long thin fingers. They were grubby after a day's picnicking, and for some reason he had a rubber band round his left wrist. They were big hands, a man's hands. The right little finger was bent outwards at a curious angle, the result of being crushed in a door when he was a child. It looked dainty, crooked for tea. I smiled, and leant forward and kissed it. He did not move.

Monsieur Joubert came in, and said the ambulance had come. He looked revived by this, but I felt emptier and more desperate.

'He'll be all right, you'll see,' he said, patting my shoulder.

Dupont came in, followed by two ambulance men. Monsieur Joubert tried to help them put Joël on the stretcher, but they waved him away in that brusque manner common to the French. In much less than a minute, the couch was empty: Joël was gone.

There's no doctor in the ambulance,' said Dupont. 'I shall have to go.' He was still in his fishing clothes. We heard him shouting at his wife, then he swept past us looking angry. His wife followed him out.

"Don't forget we have an engagement tomorrow . . .'

'Why you ever accepted that I can't think.' The ambulance doors were shut on his angry face. The ambulance drove away.

'What a man,' said Madame Dupont, her tone giving us no inkling of what she meant by that remark. She smiled vaguely and went indoors; we heard her calling the cat.

'I'll take you two girls home. They'll be wondering what on earth has happened to you.' It was after nine o'clock.

As I sat in the car on the way back it occurred to

me I could probably have gone in the ambulance too. I had never asked. I had never even thought of it. My regret and frustration were so fierce I wanted to jump out of the car and start running. What a fool, what a fool I was.

I must have made a noise, because Mic said, 'Are you all right?' I didn't answer. I had missed the opportunity to be with Joël and the pain was like a dentist drilling carelessly.

We drew up outside the Jouberts' villa.

'I forgot to drop you off,' said Monsieur in numb surprise.

'We'll walk,' said Mic.

Madame Joubert came out of the door. She looked for Joël in the car, and when she did not see him she stopped still.

'Where's Joël?' Dominique came out behind her in his pyjamas, whining. 'Be quiet and go back inside.' Woebegone, he stood still on the doorstep. His red hair glowed like Joël's.

'Where's Joël?'

Monsieur Joubert did not reply until he was out of the car. He put his arm round her shoulders and talked in a low voice. She looked sick with anxiety. Mic opened the car door, and his words became audible,

'. . . he said there were four kinds of meningitis and he wasn't sure which type Joël had, they'd have to do a final test . . .'

'If it's meningitis there's no hope . . .'

'Don't talk like that. Dupont said there was hope, although it was serious . . .'

'Doctors always say there's hope until they're proved wrong.'

They argued bitterly and pointlessly with each other until Madame burst into tears and flung her arms round her husband's neck. 'The poor boy, my poor boy,' she wailed. Dominique, frightened by his mother's tears, started to cry too. They all went inside the villa.

'Come on, let's go.' Mic looked upset. When I didn't move, she collected all our stuff together, and prodded me gently. 'Come on, stir yourself.' My legs were limp, and as we walked down the road, felt as if they belonged to someone else. My feet looked ridiculous swinging along at the end of my legs.

'I heard Marc say to Doctor Dupont that he'd be at the hospital early tomorrow morning,' said Mic. I digested this.

We reached the Menards without meeting anyone on the way. Our reception by Madame Menard was rough, and Mic immediately began shouting back at her. I escaped upstairs, unable to stand any more emotion. I curled up, shoes still on, in my Breton bed, and lay stiff and unthinking, not asleep but somehow absent. A long time later Madame's voice, soft and gentle, said behind me, 'Come and eat something. A little soup perhaps, it's very comforting.' She had brought me up a bowl of soup and bread, and an apple, and when she had gone I sat in the dark bedroom and ate. The soup was light and full of flavour, and it started my inner clock going again. I managed to get undressed and when I had climbed back into bed, I drew the curtains across and fell asleep immediately.

When I woke up it felt early; my watch had stopped during the night. I dressed quickly, and crept downstairs. It was just after half past seven, not so very early, but nobody was about. I found some milk and a piece of hard bread (French bread goes hard at once after one day) and consumed it standing up in the curtained-off kitchen. Then I hurried off down towards the Jouberts arriving there by eight. I discovered that Monsieur and Madame had already left for Rennes.

'But . . .'

Suzanne, left in charge, gave me a look implying that it was none of my business and went on preparing the children's breakfast. She added over her shoulder, 'They're going to telephone later to give us what news there is.'

176

I went and sat on the road bank. I had expected them to take me to Rennes, but it probably hadn't entered their heads. I had no claim on the family or Joël. I had been forgotten in the family crisis. I felt confused, almost wild. I wondered what on earth I would do, and blundered up the road towards the beach. When I reached the café I saw it was already open, so I went straight in. Jean was alone, wiping down the tables. He looked up in surprise when he saw it was me.

'So early?' His eyes fixed on my face. 'Come, come, it's not such a tragic world. What's the matter?'

The sight of Jean removed my numbness, and out poured my tears. 'They forgot to take me.' My words came out in a great wail. Jean walked quickly up to me and grabbed my shoulder.

'What are you talking about?'

'Joël's dying and they forgot to take me.' He shook me hard.

'You're hysterical.'

Through my distorting sobs I managed to get out, 'I'm not.'

Jean peered at me, puzzled. He had obviously not heard a word about yesterday's happenings.

'Joël was taken ill yesterday and he's gone into the hospital in Rennes.' This all came out in a rush.

'That doesn't mean he's going to *die*. Don't exaggerate.' He spoke roughly, but put his arm around me. 'What happened, did he have a bad accident?'

I shook my head, and eventually managed to say, 'He collapsed in a coma and the doctor thinks it's meningitis.'

'O la la.' Jean sounded impressed, but I got the impression that, like me, he did not know what meningitis was. 'But they'll cure him, doctors are wonderful these days. He's a strong boy.'

'It's a disease that kills if it's not caught in time.'

'You mustn't be a pessimist. He'll be back playing on the beach in no time. You'll see.' He looked im-

177

patient and uneasy when I shook my head, and went behind the bar. I sat down at a table in despair.

Antoine came in to collect his newspapers and have his breakfast, which he did every morning at Jean's.

'Ah, Antoine, cheer this young lady up. I can't do anything for her.'

'Let's give her some coffee for a start. Tell me, Mary, how's the invalid?'

So he hadn't heard the final diagnosis. I was trying to gather my voice together, when Jean said,

'If it's Joël you're talking about, she tells me he's been taken off to a hospital in Rennes, and that he's got, what was it, Mary?'

'Meningitis,' I whispered. How I hated the word.

'*Mon dieu.*' Antoine looked horrified.

'Then it's really serious?' said Jean.

'It can be a killer.'

Dust disturbed by Jean's sweeping danced in the bands of morning sun pouring obliquely through the window. Monday morning deliveries were taking place with bangs and clatters in the shop next door. Life could not have been more normal. I had to get to Rennes.

'Is there a bus to Rennes from here?'

'Of course. It goes from the village at eight-thirty.'

It was now nearly quarter to nine. No one spoke. I felt utterly hopeless.

'When's the next?'

'I think there's one in the afternoon, but not every day.'

Antoine, who was stirring his coffee abstractedly, woke up to our conversation.

'What's the problem?'

'Our little Mary wanted to go to the hospital with the Jouberts, but they left without her.'

'And the bus has gone too?'

'That's right.'

'We'll catch the bus up in my car. Let me just finish my coffee.'

In my relief at Antoine's offer I went quite faint, and felt breathless; then a desperate urge to go to the lavatory overcame me. While Antoine was making sure of the bus's route, I went. As I was washing my hands I heard through the thin door of the lobby Antoine say to Jean,

'Why is she so desperate to get to Rennes?'

'But they are in love, those two children. *C'est charmant*. They are inseparable. Antoine, you live in the world of your books and you see nothing.'

'It's true.' There was a pause during which I dried my hands and waited. 'They are very young; if that poor boy dies, she'll get over it.'

'They may be young, but they love truly. It will be hard for her.'

Antoine made a snorty noise. I came out of the cloakroom. '*Allons*,' he said. 'My car's outside.'

We caught up the bus eventually at the edge of a small town. I discovered I had no money, and Antoine gave me a handful of battered notes, some actually falling to pieces. I started to count the money but Antoine stopped me impatiently.

'Take it, take it.' He put me on the bus, and as it left I saw him standing staring after it. He looked tired and ill at ease. Perhaps he felt he had not done enough for Joël. He still hadn't got into his car when the bus turned the corner.

I sat at the back of the bus, hoping that I would be left alone. But the bus filled up; and a stout young man sat beside me, leaving me very little room. He was neat and earnest, and kept taking papers out of a black attaché case, flicking through them deftly, and putting them back. When he wasn't doing this he drummed his stubby white fingers on the lid. He tried to talk English to me, but I didn't feel in the least like casual conversation. He was a trial to me, and he was there until we reached Rennes.

When the bus set me down near, luckily, the right hospital, I stood for some time stock still, because my legs felt both weak and weighted. The journey had been a tedious unreal interlude; I now had to go and face the truth. I was mortally afraid; afraid because I did, after all, have a speck of hope Joël might live.

My progress to the hospital was slow; I had to ask the way several times, and found it hard to concentrate on the replies. When I saw the hospital my speck of hope grew bigger; surely this large efficient-looking place would be full of doctors who could save Joël. Nurses bustling by as they went off duty helped my hope to grow. Of course he would recover; what was I worrying about? This new hope filled me during all my clumsy inquiries in the foyer for the right part of the hospital. A confident young doctor, who smiled but did not bother to speak to me, took me most of the way down long corridors because his route coincided. His sleek hair, his bleeper in his pocket, his clean hands holding a file, were enough to solidify my hope. I realized as I followed him that since the moment I saw Joël lying unconscious on Dupont's couch, a heavy door had clanged in my mind, shutting off all possible futures. Now hope gave me back a sense of the future, which Joël would be part of.

The doctor pointed to an open door, and walked swiftly off, his shoes squeaking. The door led into a small waiting room, full of battered chairs and tables and overflowing ash-trays. I stopped in the doorway. The eyes of four strangers stared at me dully. I could see no Jouberts; I looked up and down the corridor, but I saw only a nurse with a trolley. For want of knowing what else to do I went into the waiting room which smelt of anxiety. Behind the open door, sitting in chairs screened earlier from my view, were Monsieur and Madame Joubert. Monsieur was leaning forward, his hands clasped between his knees. Madame, leaning back against the wall, was apparently asleep. Monsieur looked up in blank depression as I came in, and it took a few moments for my presence to register.

'Mary.'

'You forgot me.'

He stared at me without answering.

'I followed in the bus.' I sat down beside him. Madame was the other side of him, and did not move.

'I never thought of you.'

'It doesn't matter.'

He looked round at his wife. 'Still asleep. She did not sleep at all last night with worry.' He stared at her sadly. Her mouth was open, and she snored faintly.

There was a pause before I managed to ask, 'How is he?'

'He's very ill. But the doctors say there's hope. They're awaiting the results of some test.' My own hope died a little.

Monsieur Joubert sighed. 'Doctors come in here occasionally to tell us of his progress. Everyone here is waiting for news of critical cases, operations.' It was a room where anxiety, grief, even wild relief, had penetrated the very furniture. It smelt of cigarette smoke and sweat. There was an extractor fan, but it had an out-of-order notice below it.

'Where is Joël?'

'Quite near, just a few doors down.'

'Have they operated on him?'

'They don't operate on meningitis. They give him massive doses of antibiotics. The trouble is he doesn't seem to be responding very well. The doctors told me they didn't know yet what kind of meningitis he has; they did a lumbar puncture last night to take some spinal fluid for analysis, but the results are not through yet, as I told you.' All this was difficult to follow, because of the technical French, but I worked it out in retrospect, since I heard Joël's symptoms and cures gone over many times.

'Is he conscious?'

'No.'

I was intensely disappointed. Even a split second of Joël's eyes, sentient, meeting mine, would be enough.

'He's got a raging fever, he's delirious.'

Exactly twenty-four hours ago, driving through sunshine in a car full of music, I had been supremely happy. My world couldn't have changed more if an earthquake had come and demolished all the physical props of my life.

Madame Joubert opened her eyes, and sat forward yawning. Her face was tired and yellow. Without looking round she said, 'Were you talking to a doctor?'

'Mary's arrived.'

She turned to look at me. Her eyes became angry and hostile. 'What are you doing here?'

'I came to be near Joël . . .'

'Estelle.'

'This is a family tragedy. There's no place for strangers prying . . .'

'Estelle, please. She has come all the way by bus . . .'

'She can go back that way, now.' She spat the words out in a flat angry undertone; I stood up, frightened by her. 'Go. Go.'

'Estelle.' Monsieur Joubert spoke sharply. 'Be quiet. You're hysterical. Leave the child alone. She's doing no harm here.'

'I don't want strangers around at such a time. If my son dies . . .' She started to sob.

He made me sit down before he put his arms round his wife. She sobbed, dry shuddering sobs. He said over her head, 'She's never been strong in a crisis. Don't mind her, she really doesn't mean the things she said.'

And indeed, when the sobbing fit was over, Madame took my hand, smiled at me, and said in kind though distracted tones, 'Good girl, good girl.'

We sat for a long time in silence. Then a rattling trolley appeared and we bought drink and food off it. I was ravenously hungry, so were the Jouberts; we all gobbled greedily. By this time the waiting room was empty, so we no longer spoke in undertones. This and food inside us made us feel more normal. Madame began to talk about Joël; once she started she talked compulsively, about the illnesses he had had, about his special problems, about every aspect of him. Her mind hopped about. Sometimes what she said made me feel we knew two different boys. The one I knew was more vivid and humorous.

'He always liked girls,' said Madame. 'It's true, isn't it, Marc? Ever since he was a little boy his best friends were always girls.'

'You make him sound soft,' said her husband crossly. 'What about Matthieu. He does everything with Matthieu.'

'But now Matthieu's transferred to the Lycée Henri Quatre they don't see much of each other.'

Monsieur shrugged. Some aspect of the conversation annoyed him, but he smiled at his wife as if to hide this. She fiddled with the cross round her neck.

Quick firm steps came a short way down the corridor and turned into the waiting room. A doctor smiled in recognition at the Jouberts.

'You've had a long wait, I'm afraid, and no news. 'We've now got the results of the tests and we know what kind of meningitis your son has.' He hesitated. It was impossible to guess anything from his frank-looking blue eyes. 'His condition is not good, not good at all. Various unfortunate complications have set in. If only he had been brought to us earlier, and the antibiotic treatment started hours before.' His bleeper started, but he switched it off.

I felt very cold.

Madame said in an uneven voice, 'Then you're trying to tell us there's no hope?'

'While a human being still lives, there is always hope.'

Madame sat rubbing the fingers of one hand repeatedly with the other. '*Ah, non,*' she said. '*Ah, non. Ce n'est pas juste.*' She looked a little crazy.

'Would you like to come and sit with your son? It may give you comfort.'

Madame and Monsieur leapt to their feet, and so did I. I was going in with them if I had to fight my way in. I had missed too much already. No one in fact took any notice of me.

Joël's red hair was a mass of flames on the pillow. His face was wasted and feverish. His body looked very long in the hospital bed. He had a whitish grey hospital nightshirt on.

The doctor's bleeper started up again. 'I'll be back soon,' he said to the nurse in attendance. She was a solid taciturn woman who filled the small room with her presence. She never smiled, and having looked us over once with bored cold eyes, ignored us. Madame Joubert sat on the only chair; Monsieur and I stood. I tried to get up near him but the nurse waved me back. She stood, literally and figuratively, between me and Joël, and I knew she would win. As I stared desperately at her, I named her mentally the Angel of Death. She was plump, and from the back view kindly and comforting. But her face knew neither of these qualities; it was round and flat, with a curious spread nose as if someone, impatient with his handiwork, had squashed her nose in with his palm. Her mouth was a small tight trap, and she talked without showing her teeth. She hardly lifted her eyes at all to look at you; when she did they were just cold blank grey jelly. She filled the room with an aura of evil, and it seemed to explain why Joël was not recovering. How could he; she was anti-life.

I expect my state of mind has made me exaggerate this woman; I don't know. She has haunted me ever since, and if I ever saw her flat cold face again she would fill me with terror. When the priest came to give Joël Extreme Unction, she stood in the corner, her eyes down; but her presence seemed to cancel out the priest's. Soon after this Joël opened his eyes. I pushed past the nurse and stood against the bed. He saw his parents and obviously recognized them; his green eyes lit up. After a few moments his eyelids started to close again. I had to meet those eyes; I leant forward

184

into his line of vision and touched his cheek. His eyes swung round and he saw me.

'My Mary,' he whispered. His eyes smiled.

Joël died not long after midnight, without further regaining consciousness. By that time the Angel of Death was off duty.

II

My father offered to come and fetch me himself. He sounded surprised when I said, 'No, I'd like to stay here for a while.'

'Oh, well, ring me again if you change your mind.'

I admit that my first reaction had been to rush back to England away from reminders of Joël. But by the end of a morning wandering by myself along the cliffs, my face swollen and red, I saw that painful though these familiar reminders were, my raw grief would be worse away from them.

Joël was buried in the graveyard of the beautiful inappropriately large church at Tréguinec. The church was full; all the villagers, and all the families *en vacance* came, and even some stray holiday-makers. Jean closed his café to come. It was a hot day, and the church smelt of summer throughout the service. Children whispered and people wept. I saw the cold sophisticated woman who ran the clothes boutique with tears running down her face. Everyone mourns a life cut off before it had really begun. Though I did not weep at this public ceremony, I found my grief had acquired two levels, for the tragic waste of his death, and for my own special loss.

I was comforted by the ordinary daily round at Tréguinec. We spent days on the beach, we played ping-pong, we passed a normal holiday existence. The

Jouberts stayed on too, rather to my surprise, I think for the same reasons as I did. They would arrive on the beach in a family group, which they never did before. Suzanne, Marcel, Emmanuelle, Dominique, Pish in her mother's arms; arriving together, they emphasized that there was one missing. There seemed to be a gap in the air somewhere amongst them, a powerful vacuum that drew the eyes and disappointed them by not manifesting itself. The little ones had not grasped the finality of what had happened, but Suzanne and Marcel looked pinched with heartache. I noticed tears coursing down Suzanne's cheeks as if, as mine did, they overflowed every so often for a minute or two, with no change of facial expression. Once Suzanne and I collided with each other on a small path hidden on the cliffs; we stared at each other, tears filling our eyes, and then hugged each other briefly before running off in separate directions. It was the only time either of us openly acknowledged the other's grief.

One cold windy afternoon I was in no mood to play ping-pong with Mic, and instead I walked off towards the Baron's property. It was a Tuesday, exactly a week after Joël death. I had a strong desire to leave Tréguinec as soon as possible; it had propped me long enough. I walked briskly up the unmade road as far as the white gate which used to be kept bolted; it was hanging open now. I wondered whether the Baron was enjoying prison. His life had fallen to pieces with the suddenness mine had. For him there was an end to prison. My life would never get back what it had lost.

The Baron's grounds were weedy and untidy; people had picnicked, leaving the usual litter behind. I reached the helicopter landing field, where the dolmen had once been. The grass was thick, and no longer blown flat in swathes by the wind from the choppers. It was desolate. The wind whined in the gorse bushes. I stood in the middle, the likely site of the dolmen, and it seemed I heard our own giggling voices when Joël,

Mic and I grew hysterical with laughter on this spot that night last year.

After a while I started to walk round the edges of the area, trying to see where the great stones of the dolmen had been disposed of. Even if they had been dynamited surely there would be some evidence of this. I pushed through the undergrowth towards the cliff. At one place the cliff edge had fallen away, like the crumbling lip of a quarry. Falls of stone lay all down the sides; large boulders at the bottom. Here were the dolmen stones, easy to pick out because they had weathered rounded planes ending in jagged edges. They were broken past saving, it seemed to me. I thought of the hands that had chipped away until the stones were the right shape, and somehow lifted those huge stones to form the dolmen. The Baron had undone it in a day.

That evening at supper I told Monsieur Menard that I had found the stones. He had only arrived from Paris the preceding day, having been unable to come down before because he was involved in a state visit of the American president.

'Poor little dolmen,' he said. 'You must show me. One day I'll have that man prosecuted.' But I got the impression he knew as well as I did that day would somehow never come. As if to cover this up, he talked with great enthusiasm and knowledge about megaliths. They were clearly of genuine interest to him.

'An English professor has found out some fascinating facts about these Stone Age megaliths. He said your great stone circle at Avebury was set out with an accuracy of one in a thousand; but subsequently he discovered that the alignment of the stones at Carnac have an even greater accuracy.' He thought we looked insufficiently impressed, so he explained. 'This is the sort of accuracy rare even in modern engineering; the accuracy needed in working out, say, the effects of heat expansion on a steel tape. Minute accuracy.'

Gervaise whistled. Even Mic looked interested.

'How on *earth* could they do it?' I said. This talk of

prehistoric precision was the first thing that drove grief fully from my mind for a short space. I marvelled; bare hands, huge stones, rough soggy ground. How indeed had they done it.

'It seems Stone Age man knew his geometry.'

'Who did you say found this out?'

'I forget his name. Professor something. I'll look it up when I get back to Paris, and send it to you.'

'You don't need to bother . . .'

'No, no, of course I will. After all, he may teach in an English university and if your interest continues, it's possible you might want to study under him. It's always as well to note down the names of people who make discoveries that interest you.'

Archaeology; it was not a new possibility. Deep inside me I felt a stirring of hope in the future, of life holding promise again.

The next morning I went for a walk with Monsieur Menard—he wanted me to show him the broken dolmen stones.

'I'm sorry you're leaving us tomorrow. There won't be time for a trip to Carnac.'

'No. I—I needn't go yet, but I can't face Tréguinec any more.'

'I quite understand. It has been a tragic and upsetting time for everyone, but apart from Joël's family, for you especially.' The sound of Joël's name in the air hurt me, yet Monsieur said it in a cool detached way that was also a relief. I said nothing; I did not trust my voice. He went on as if he did not expect me to speak. 'There is something unreal about a sudden death, something very hard to come to terms with. A disease descends upon a young person and kills him. Why? Why him? It seems the pettish action of a bored creator who wants to liven things up for the hell of it. If Joël had been killed in a car smash, we would have felt rage against a tragic waste. As it is we feel cheated. Man did not kill him, and man could do nothing to save him. We feel cheated.'

It was true. I felt cheated, cosmically cheated. Tears ran down my face. Monsieur saw them falling, but took no special notice of them.

'A profound thing has happened to you, of great importance to your future.'

'If Joël had lived it would have been more important.' I ached with grief.

Monsieur Menard shrugged. 'Perhaps. Perhaps not.'

Through my grief came anger. 'How can you say that? Life is always better than death.'

'I can say it, Mary, because I am thirty years older than you. I may be wrong, of course, because contrary to what most adults seem to believe, I don't hold that experience necessarily brings wisdom. Experience does however give one the confidence to talk *about* experience. *Ecoute-moi, ma fille.* In my own life I've learned this: dreadful things can turn out as time passes to be the most valuable things that ever happened to you. Anyone with experience can tell you that.' He paused. I felt exhausted, wrung out. 'And here is another, rarer truth. The essential factor that makes life beautiful and significant is death. Eternal life would be a nightmare. Only death makes living valuable.'

I did not want to listen to him or think any more. His words hid themselves in my brain, and came to the surface many times later on. Now we walked on in silence, his thoughtful, mine caused by an overwhelming sense of loss which crept into every corner of my being. Nothing in my week of grief had prepared me for this. I thought I would faint, but somehow we reached the field, and pushed our way through the undergrowth to the edge of the cliff. Monsieur looked at the broken stones and we went home again in silence.

At the Menards' I found a battered duffle bag on my bed. Mic was sitting in the adjoining room, writing. She turned when she heard me.

'Estelle Joubert brought those for you. They've left

Tréguinec and gone back to Paris. She said they would probably finish the *vacances* in Calais with their grandmother.'

I stood still, gazing at Mic.

'You've just missed them. They came to say goodbye.'

'They didn't say they were going today.'

'They decided suddenly last night.'

I picked up the bag; it was the one Joël had brought with him to London. It was stuffed full. I could not bear to pull anything out in Mic's presence, so I put the bag half out of sight behind the curtains of my Breton bed. Mic finished the letter she was writing, put it in a crackling envelope, and left the cottage to post it. I heard her whistling as she went out of the gate. As far as I could tell from the quiet, everyone was out.

At the top of the duffle bag was the large red-and-white striped sweater of Joël's I had put on the evening he fell ill. It had been washed, but still smelt of Joël's skin. I held it against my face.

Beneath the sweater was a red-and-white cotton scarf, wrapped round some nobbly objects. I unwrapped it. Inside was a frog like mine made of limpet shells, Joël's fountain pen, and a small leather photograph holder with a blurred snap of me in it. There was also a tin soldier, part of a set I had noticed on a shelf in the caravan. I suppose the others were given to his brothers and sisters. The scarf was of the softest Indian cotton.

At the bottom of the bag, under a copy of *Le Grand Meaulnes,* with his name in it, and a copy belonging to me of *Catcher in the Rye* which he had borrowed in London, was a large bundle of letters; all my letters to Joël. He had numbered and dated each one on its envelope; they were tied up with thick green tape. Like him, I had brought all his letters with me to Tréguinec. Mine were all stuffed into a shoebag. I got them out, and put his and my letters into order, one answering the other, until our dialogue was complete.